# QUEEN?

**5.** *The party is rockin'. Are you the first to:*

a) Turn up the music and start grooving round the room?

b) Say you think it must be time for everyone to go home?

c) Play a silly game like Twister?

**6.** *It's time for "Truth or Dare". Tick the ones you'd be willing to do:*

a) Get down on the floor on all fours and pretend you're a dog.

b) Mimic someone in the room.

c) Sing a Robbie song backwards.

**7.** *After the party, back at school, would your mates:*

a) Talk about the party nonstop?

b) Just mention it in passing?

c) Avoid you?

## 1 - 10
*What a party pooper!*
Oh dear, oh dear! You really need to learn how to chill out and enjoy yourself! If you don't, you'll never really have a successful or fun party.

## 11 - 20
*You're a party princess!*
Your mates are probably queueing up to get an invite to your parties! You *love* having fun and you can laugh at yourself, too!

## 21 - 29
*You wear the crown of the party queen!*
You are totally *mad* about parties! But try not to be the centre of attention all the time or your crown will soon slip!

# what's in?

56

106

74

52

34

108

126

Printed and Published in Great Britain by D. C. THOMSON & CO. LTD.,
185 Fleet Street, London EC4A 2HS. © D. C. THOMSON & CO. LTD., 2002.
ISBN 0 85116 811 6

Vicky Mills' big brother Matt was at university.

**BIG BROTHER**

That was Matt on the phone. He's bringing his girlfriend, Holly, home for Christmas.

Wow! He must be keen!

The trouble is, she's a vegetarian. Matt's asked if we can go without the turkey for dinner this Christmas.

What? We *always* have turkey for Christmas dinner!

I haven't a clue what to cook instead.

Can't you just give her a Quorn burger or something, Mum? Then we can still have turkey?

No. Matt says that even *looking* at meat makes Holly feel sick.

Huh! And she's making *me* feel sick. Mum should refuse to have her!

It's difficult, but Holly is Matt's friend so I think we should respect her views.

What about *our* views? Obviously Matt doesn't care about those!

Vicky told her mate, Tricia —

She sounds a pain. Pity I can't do like they do in the Big Brother programme and vote her out of the house.

Yeah, I know what you mean. My sister Ros is going out with a right dork now. It was much better when she was dating your brother.

Yes it was, wasn't it? Pity we can't get them back together again.

I'll work on it, Tricia. Leave it to me.

I'm all for it. The best Chrissie pressie you could give me is getting Ros to give grotty Glenn the heave.

The next day —

Come on, Vicky, give me a hand, will you? They'll be here any minute.

Honestly, Mum, I don't know why you're making such a fuss. Holly's only Matt's *girlfriend!*

6

That's not the point. Clear away that mess, will you?

Okay, okay!

So —

This is Holly, everyone.

Hello.

Hi.

I suppose I'd better be civil.

I understand you're a vegetarian, Holly. I want to organise a special Christmas dinner. So what would you like?

Quorn fillets would be lovely, Mrs Mills. And I don't mind if the rest of you have turkey. Looking at meat used to make me feel ill, but I'm over that now!

Wow! We can have turkey. Nice one, Holly. Perhaps you're not such a pain!

## And things got even better —

I'll show you an easy way to tune up. Watch.

Great. Thanks, Holly. Matt said he'd do it for me before he went to uni in September but he never got round to it!

I play in a band at college, Vicky. This is a really easy riff. I'll show you, then you can have a go.

She's great. I 't believe this. A itar lesson, too.

## But Matt didn't like them getting on too well—

Let's go and watch a video together, Holly. You're here to see me, remember.

Sorry, bro. I didn't realise she was your exclusive property!

7

Actually, Holly is really great. But how do I tell Tricia that I'd rather Matt went out with Holly than her big sister? Me and my big mouth!

How was your Christmas dinner, Vicky? Did you have nut roast or something?

No, erm, actually we had turkey. Holly didn't mind. She had Quorn.

So it wasn't too bad then?

This is awful. I don't know what to say and Tricia seems a bit off, too.

Look, Vic, we'll have to call off our matchmaking thing. Ros got engaged to Glenn over Christmas. They're getting married in June.

Really?

Phew, what a relief!

How do you feel about it?

Fine, actually. I got to know him a bit over Christmas. He's a good laugh when he gets going. And I'm going to be a bridesmaid!

Sorry I can't help with offloading Holly.

That's okay. Actually I like too, so it's turned out ok

8

Good job Tricia didn't have to know I preferred Holly to Ros. I wonder how long she'll be staying? Be good if it's until New Year. She might even show me some more riffs.

But —

Don't ask!

Hi, Matt. Where's Holly?

Huh? What's going on here?

I'm afraid they had a bit of a row and Holly's broken it off. She went home half an hour ago. Seems she thought your brother was a bit too possessive.

Nice one, Matt. You get yourself a really brilliant girlfriend and you blow it. I wish I could vote *you* out of the house now!

Mum filled her in —

Oh, no!

# THE END

9

# The Comp

IT'S YOUR SISTER ON THE PHONE, ROZ. SHE SAYS IT'S IMPORTANT.
WHAT? CARLY? IN LA? I HOPE NOTHING'S WRONG!
MOM'S GETTING *MARRIED* AGAIN? REALLY? I DIDN'T EVEN KNOW SHE HAD A BOYFRIEND!
IT'S ALL HAPPENED REAL QUICKLY. THEY MET AT SOME WORK PARTY AND IT JUST WENT FROM THERE. BUT I LIKE GUY. HE'S COOL.
BRILLIANT. YOU'LL HAVE TO SEND ME A PICCIE, CARLY. I CAN'T WAIT TO SEE WHAT HE LOOKS LIKE!

At school —

GUESS WHAT? MOM'S GETTING MARRIED AGAIN. HIS NAME'S GUY AND CARLY SAYS HE'S DEAD COOL!

WICKED, ROZ. DOES HE LIVE IN BEVERLY HILLS?

IS HE A FILM DIRECTOR?

NO, SHE MET HIM THROUGH HER WORK. BUT I DON'T MIND WHAT HE DOES. I'M JUST REAL HAPPY FOR MOM.

But there was more excitement to come —

GUY AND I HAVE DECIDED TO GET MARRIED IN LAS VEGAS, ROZ. I'D LOVE YOU TO BE MY BRIDESMAID WITH CARLY. YOU CAN BRING A FRIEND WITH YOU — AT OUR EXPENSE.

COOL! I'LL ASK HAYLEY. SHE'LL BE FREAKED! THANKS, MOM. I'LL PHONE HER RIGHT AWAY.

But —

WAIT A MINUTE! HAYLEY'LL BE COOL AT THE THOUGHT OF A FREE TRIP TO VEGAS, BUT BECKY'LL BE DEAD UPSET. THEY ARE TWINS, AFTER ALL.

MAYBE I SHOULD ASK STANCEE IT WOULDN'T BE MUCH FUN, BUT SHE IS MY STEP-SISTER. OH I DUNNO WHAT TO DO.

THAT'S YOUR MOTHER ON THE PHONE AGAIN, ROZ.

OH, THANKS, CATHY.

CARLY'S JUST REMINDED ME THAT HAYLEY HAS A TWIN SISTER. YOU CAN HARDLY ASK ONE AND NOT THE OTHER, SO JUST GO AHEAD AND ASK THEM BOTH, OKAY?

YOU BET! THANKS, MOM. THAT'S MY PROBLEM SOLVED!

POOR STANCEE. STILL, SHE NEVER KNEW HOW CLOSE SHE CAME TO THE TRIP OF A LIFETIME.

The girls decided to do some serious shopping.

MOM'S GETTING CARLY AND ME SPECIAL OUTFITS FOR THE CEREMONY, BUT I'LL NEED LOADS OF NEW STUFF.

THAT TOP'S GREAT, ROZ.

GO FOR IT.

Roz showed Cathy what she had bought.

THESE ARE NICE, EH, STANCEE?

YEAH! YOU — YOU MUST BE DEAD EXCITED.

POOR STANCEE. I CAN'T HELP FEELING A BIT SORRY FOR HER.

I KNOW WHAT YOU MEAN. BUT YOU COULD HARDLY INVITE YOUR DAD'S NEW WIFE'S DAUGHTER TO YOUR MUM'S WEDDING.

At last the time came to fly out —

YOU CERTAIN YOU'LL BE OKAY NOW, GIRLS?

SURE, DAD. GUY AND MOM ARE MEETING US IN LA. AND WE'VE CHECKED IN, SO WHAT ELSE CAN GO WRONG?

But, ten minutes later —

I LEFT MY BAG HERE, HONESTLY!

OKAY. LET'S JUST RETRACE OUR STEPS.

# Information

Half an hour later —

IT WAS HANDED IN BY SECURITY. DON'T LEAVE ANY BAGGAGE UNATTENDED AGAIN, PLEASE.

SORRY, WE WON'T.

LET'S GO TO DEPARTURE NOW — BEFORE ANYTHING *ELSE* GOES WRONG.

But then, in the toilet —

THE DOOR'S STUCK. I CAN'T GET OUT.

KEEP TRYING, HAYLEY. I'LL GET HELP.

OUR FLIGHT'S BEEN CALLED! THIS IS A DISASTER.

But, eventually —

QUICK, OR IT'LL GO WITHOUT US!

WAIT FOR US, MR PILOT! WE'RE COMING THROUGH!

And —

ROZ! IT'S LOVELY TO SEE YOU. HI, GIRLS.

HI!

MEET GUY, EVERYONE.

HI, GIRLS, AND WELCOME TO LA. SORRY I CAN'T HANG AROUND, BUT I'VE GOTTA WORK TODAY. I'LL SEE YOU ALL IN VEGAS.

OKAY, GUY.

WOW! HE LOOKS LIKE A FILM STAR.

AND HE SEEMS DEAD NICE. CARLY SAID HE WAS COOL, AND FOR ONCE SHE WAS RIGHT.

CHEEK!

14

Next day —

BETTER MAKE THE MOST OF THIS REST, GIRLS. IT'LL BE ALL GO WHEN WE SET OFF FOR VEGAS ON FRIDAY.

IT'LL BE COOL, MOM. I CAN'T WAIT.

And soon —

WOW! JUST LOOK AT EVERYTHING! IT'S WILD! I'VE SEEN THIS ON TV, BUT I NEVER IMAGINED ANYTHING SO . . . BIG!

The hotel was huge, too.

LOOK AT THIS. PLUSH OR WHAT?

AND BECKY AND HAYLEY HAVE THE SUITE NEXT DOOR.

THIS IS AMAZING, ROZ. I CAN'T WAIT FOR THE WEDDING NOW.

LET'S LOOK ROUND VEGAS FIRST, HAYLEY!

HOW DO YOU LIKE ALL THIS, ROZ?

IT'S GREAT, MOM. I'LL NEVER FORGET IT!

AND YOU DO LIKE GUY, DON'T YOU? YOU DO APPROVE!

YEAH! HE SEEMS REALLY NICE, MOM. OF COURSE I APPROVE.

15

Tired of the same old Christmas cards year after year? Then why not make your own? It's simple - and lots and lots of fun!

# ...make...m

## What you'll need :

A selection of coloured card

Sequins and charms (available from craft shops)

Shiny wrapping paper

Scissors

Glue

To make the basic card, choose a colour and decide what size you'd like your card to be. One of the advantages of making your own cards is that you can have them any size you want - as long as you make sure you have an envelope to fit. Also remember to cut the card twice as wide as you want it to be as it will be folded over.

Once you have cut your card, score gently down the middle to make folding over easier, then carefully fold in half. Decide what decorations you would like on the front, then lay them in place to see what they look like before you finally glue them down. Be careful when gluing to put only enough glue on the charm or sequin and not to spread too much over the card as it will spoil the look of the finished card. It's as simple as that.

# e...make...make...

Here's how we decorated some of ours - but feel free to experiment.

A pale blue card sprinkled with silver snowflakes looks really effective.

Four gold cherubs or some Christmas bells look really festive when placed at different angles around a large gold snowflake.

Try placing a large gold star with a 'tail' of smaller stars on a dark blue card. It looks like a comet against a dark blue sky.

Use a template of thicker card to cut a simple Christmas tree shape from shiny paper, then top with a gold star. This looks really nice on a pale green card.

And there's no need to waste any pieces of leftover coloured card, cos they can be turned into great labels for your Crimbo parcels. You can make them to match your cards, or completely different. It's up to you.

Cut Christmas trees as before, but this time put two on the front of your tall, pale coloured card. To make this one extra special, we've put a sprinkling of small gold stars on the inside of the card.

19

# Switched On!

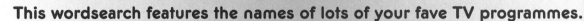

How eagle-eyed are you?
This wordsearch features the names of lots of your fave TV programmes.
The titles are listed below and they can read up, down,
backwards, forwards and diagonally. The letters
can be used more than once.

T E J T A E B T R A E H L
H O L L Y O A K S N M O D
E M P B E L A D R E M M E
S A F O X S T A R T R E K
I E S Y F R I E N D S A E
M T A T S T A R G U R N D
P A B L E G H T Q H A D I
S D R A U N W E N G E A S
O D I U R K D O P R Y W K
N N S B C Y E N O S A O
N N S J I M A R T P Y O
S I A A J I M A R T P Y O
O L T C O P P W K S U S R
F B E I R E T E P E U L B

BLUE PETER
STAR TREK ✓
FRIENDS ✓

RUGRATS ✓
BLIND DATE ✓
THE SIMPSONS
HOME AND AWAY
TOP OF THE POPS
CASUALTY ✓

EMMERDALE
SABRINA
BROOKSIDE ✓
HEARTBEAT ✓
EASTENDERS ✓
HOLLYOAKS ✓

20

# The Four Marys

MARY FIELD, Mary Cotter, Mary Radleigh and Mary Simpson were in the Third Form at St Elmo's School for Girls, and were best friends. One afternoon —

PARENTS' DAY TOMORROW. I CAN'T WAIT TO SEE MY FOLKS!

SAME HERE, COTTY. DAD'S CAR'S IN THE GARAGE AGAIN, SO HE AND MUM WILL HAVE TO GET THE TRAIN.

IMAGINE ONLY HAVING *ONE* CAR IN THE FAMILY, MABEL.

THEY'RE ONLY COMMON PEOPLE, VERONICA. I'M SURPRISED THEY DON'T *CYCLE* OVER.

OOH! THOSE SNOBS!

IGNORE THEM, FIELDY. I DO!

IS YOUR BROTHER COMING TOMORROW, MABEL?

YES. HE'S GOING TO ST BARTOPH'S, SO MUMMY AND DADDY WILL TAKE HIM THERE AFTERWARDS.

*TWO* LENTHAMS IN ONE TOWN! I'M NOT SURE ELMBURY CAN STAND IT!

YOU'RE RIGHT THERE, RADDY.

21

OF COURSE, DAVID, YOU DO REALISE THAT MARY SIMPSON TELLS HER SILLY FRIENDS EVERYTHING ABOUT YOUR DATES?

IT UPSETS US TO HAVE TO TELL YOU, DAVID, BUT WE DON'T LIKE TO HEAR THEM MAKING FUN OF YOU . . .

OH, I'LL SURVIVE. BUT I GET THE FEELING YOU TWO DON'T LIKE MARY MUCH!

IT — IT'S NOT SO MUCH THAT, DAVID. BUT HER PARENTS ARE — WELL — COMMON!

SO WAS OUR DAD — UNTIL HE MADE A LOT OF MONEY OUT OF HIS BUILDER'S BUSINESS.

HOW DARE YOU COMPARE OUR FATHER TO . . . TO . . . WELL, REALLY!

IF WE CAN'T PUT DAVID OFF SIMPSON, WE'LL HAVE TO PUT *HER* OFF *HIM!*

So —

DAVID'S HAD ANOTHER LONG LETTER FROM SHELLEY, HIS GIRLFRIEND BACK HOME. HE MISSES HER SO MUCH, VERONICA — HE WRITES TO HER *EVERY* DAY.

24

25

# Pssst!

## wanna know some stars' secrets?

**David Beckham** has two middle names - Robert and Joseph.

**Sandi allSTARS** just lurves strawberry ice cream!

**Tash** from **Atomic Kitten** is a huge Easties fan.

**Britney** would love to make a movie like Grease!

**Destiny's Child** say one of their best moments was being invited to **Whitney Houston's** birthday party.

**Bradley S Club 7** was fired from Pizza Hut when he was younger because he spent too much time looking at the girlies.

A skiing trip was **Ashley allSTARS** best ever Christmas present.

When **Bethany Platt** was born in Coronation Street, identical twins Amy and Emily Walton were chosen to play her.

**Emma Bunton** and **Tina S Club 7** both appeared in the same TV ad when they were younger.

Footballer **Michael Owen** was born in Chester - that's where Hollyoaks is set.

Recognise the girl on this page? Of course you do, she's the cover girl from this year's Bunty Annual. But is being a cover model as much fun as it sounds? Read on and find out what life as a model is really like!

First of all you should register with a model agency. This means your photograph will appear in a catalogue which will be sent out to possible hirers - like the people who produce this book.

When we are looking for girls as possible cover models we look through lots of different model catalogues before deciding which models we want to use.

On the day of the cover shoot there is usually the model, her chaperone, a stylist who brings the clothes, a make up artist, a hairdresser and, last but certainly not least, the photographer. Sometimes there are assistants too, who help things to run more smoothly. You might imagine that a photographer's studio would be a glamorous place, but in reality most are big, open spaces with very little furniture. Changing facilities are sometimes small, too, so there isn't much room for the model to get in and out of the various outfits she will be asked to wear.

The model doesn't usually have any choice about what she wears either, as the stylist will have decided on the outfits before the shoot begins. And neither does she get to keep the clothes when the shoot is over.

es right! • eyes left! • smile! • that's it! • say cheese! • chin up! • eyes right! • eyes left! • smile!

Sometimes models do complain about having to wear certain styles or colours, but in general they accept what they are given. After all, it's a job and they are being paid.

Once the make up and hair are done, it is time for the photographer to take charge. He or she will tell the model where to stand or sit and will, throughout the shoot, give the model instructions to move one way, then the other, then to hold her head a bit higher or lower. It's not easy.

All the time this is going on, the stylist, make up artist and hairdresser are on hand, ready to touch up make up, re-comb hair or tuck in a label or strap. And what does the model do? She keeps smiling. No matter how uncomfortable her clothes are, or if they are held together with pins or clips at the back, she just has to keep smiling. And, as a cover shoot can take anything from two to three hours, depending how many outfits are being used, she has to have patience and stamina.

All in all, the photographer will take at least twelve shots of any one outfit, and the choice of which one appears will be up to the editor of the magazine or book.

So do you still think it would be glamorous to be a cover model? It's certainly not easy - but it's fun all the same.

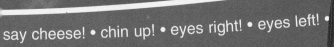

say cheese! • chin up! • eyes right! • eyes left! •

# Rosie & co

Hi, I'm Rosie. That's me wearing the stripy top. The others are my best friends Melanie, Jenny T and Jenny M. We always do everything together. Well, up until last summer that is.

It had been a strange holiday. None of us was going away until autumn, so we seemed to have been hanging around trying to think of things to do for weeks on end. If the truth be told, we were beginning to get on each other's nerves.

"I vote we go to the leisure centre," Jenny T suggested for the fourth time that week. "There's a new water slide opening and it sounds cool!"

"Give it a rest, Jen!" Melanie sighed. "You know I hate swimming! I vote we go to the mall and do some shopping!"

"What with?" groaned Jenny M. "I dunno about you, but I'm broke. There's no way I could afford to go shopping."

And I was the same. I couldn't afford to go shopping and, like Melanie, didn't really fancy the leisure centre. In fact, I couldn't understand why Jenny T was so keen. She normally wasn't wild about swimming, either.

"You can count me out, too," I started to say. "I...

"Okay, then," Jenny T go up crossly. "We just sit around here for another da do we? Well, you lot can suit yourself, but I'm going out." And with that she stomped out of the room and down the stairs.

❀ ❀ ❀ ❀

"Ooops!" Melanie grinne as we heard the outside door closing with a thump.

What now?"

"Well, we can't hang 'round here!" I said, 'etting to my feet. "It's enny T's house, remember? f she goes, we go!"

Downstairs we shouted 'bye" to Mrs T and made 'ur separate ways home.

❁ ❁ ❁ ❁

All that night I expected 'enny to phone, but there 'as nothing. I was a bit 'pset, really, cos we'd 'ever fallen out like that 'efore, and I didn't want 'e squabble to go on.

"Is it okay if I call Jenny T 'the morning?" I asked 'lum later. "We had a bit 'f a fall out earlier, and I 'ant to make sure she's 'kay."

"Fine," Mum grinned. 'Just don't take too long."

But when I called the next 'ay, Jenny wasn't in!

"She's gone to the leisure 'entre," her mum told me. 'I thought she was meeting 'ou all there."

'I stammered a bit, but I 'idn't want to land Jenny in 'rouble, so I muttered 'omething about having 'rgotten and hung up. 'What on earth was going 'n? Why had Jenny said 'e was with us when she 'asn't? I had to find out 'e truth, so I got on the

phone to Jenny M and Melanie right away.

"Emergency meeting needed!" I said to them both. "Meet me in the park beside the school in fifteen minutes."

The others were as puzzled as me by Jenny T's behaviour.

"She's been a bit odd for the last couple of days," Melanie said, "but it's not like her to be quite as touchy as she was yesterday."

"You're right," Jenny M agreed. "Let's go into the centre and find out what's going on."

But we hadn't even reached the gates of the park when Melanie let out a shout!

"There she is. And - and look who she's with!"

Sure enough, Jenny T was standing near the park gate, hand in hand with Richard French. And who's Richard French? Only the school pin-up boy, that's who! We couldn't believe it.

As we watched, they spoke for a while then Richard went off towards the bus stop. Jenny turned - and that's when she spotted us.

"I - I suppose you're wondering what's going on,"

she looked embarrassed as she approached.

"Yeah!" I grinned. "Spill the beans, Jen. How long has this been going on"?"

"Today was our first sort of date," she said shyly. "Richard phoned me last weekend and asked if I wanted to go down to the leisure centre. His big brother's a lifeguard and Rich has been sort of helping out during the holidays. I was too embarrassed to go on my own - that's why I wanted you lot to come with me. When you wouldn't I was really mad cos I thought I'd miss out."

"But why didn't you say?" Melanie was amazed. "Even I would have come swimming with you if I'd known you were going to be meeting Richard French! Wow!"

Jenny T giggled. "He is gorgeous, isn't he? And he's dead nice, too. Anyway, I was so mad at you lot that I decided to pluck up my courage and go to meet Richard on my own. And I'm glad I did. We're meeting again tomorrow and he's asked me to go to the cinema with him on Friday! Impressed?"

Were we impressed? You

bet we were. But I was still a bit worried about why Jenny had lied to her mum.

❁ ❁ ❁ ❁

"I didn't lie," she explained when I asked. "Mum knew I was meeting Richard, but she thought I was meeting you lot, too. I - I didn't make her any wiser in case she didn't want me going on my own."

"But she wouldn't have bothered," Jenny M said. "Your mum's cool, Jenny."

"I suppose you're right. I'll tell her when I get home," Jenny T grinned. "Anyway, now you see why I was so keen on us going to the leisure centre."

And we did see. Right there and then we made a pact. If any one of us wanted the others to help out with a date or anything, we would just say so.

"But promise me one thing," Jenny T said seriously.

"Anything!" we said, desperate to make up for almost ruining things for our friend.

"Don't turn up on Friday, when we go to the cinema! That's one time I don't want you around! Understand?"

We did!

# It's in the STARS!

If you're Aries, Taurus or Gemini, then right here's the place to check out what's in store for 2003.

## Aries

### (March 21 - April 20)

Your lucky colour is bright red, so wear it lots - especially in the first few months of 2003. A change of class at school could bring new friendships later in the year, and a person born in December or March could turn out to be extra special. Sounds exciting, doesn't it?

**Star Special**

Loadsa bright nail polish! The wilder the better! Wow!

**Hot Hobby** Acting or dancing

## Taurus

### (April 21 - May 20)

October is often a lucky month for you and this year it could be even better than usual. Hard work at school always pays off and a reward could well be coming your way. Don't be tempted to spend too much in the first half of the year, cos you could need your money later.

**Star Special**

Anything that glitters! Go for it!

**Hot Hobby** Music or gymnastics

## Gemini

### (May 21 - June 21)

Travel looks like being important to you this year. A special holiday, perhaps - or even a move away. A new hobby looks very interesting, but find out a bit about it before you get too involved. You may not have enough time to do everything you'd like, tempting though it may be.

**Star Special**

Books, books, books! You read anything!

**Hot Hobby** Art and reading

turn to page 64 for more stars.

# 25 Cool Christma

## It just wouldn't be Christmas without these f

### DISCO
Time to paaarty! Get all glittered up, girlies!

### HOLLY
It looks great but has to be handled with care!

### TREE
It's never really Christmas until you've decorated your tree!

### SNOW
Make a snowman, throw snowballs, let snowflakes melt on your tongue!

### ICE
Check out its fab patterns on windows and puddles.

### ADVENT CALENDARS
Count down to Christmas, chomping chocolate as you go! How cool!

### CARDS
The more, the merrier! make them yourself, covered with glitter!

### SANTA
Ho! Ho! Ho! EVERYONE loves Santa!

### ROBIN
Isn't this just the cutest little bird?

### STAR
A twinkly, sparkly topping to your Christmas tree!

### MISTLETOE
Ready, steady, go! Chase after EVERYONE you fancy!

### TINSEL
Wear it in your hair to the school disco! Or tie it around your pressies.

# things!

...stive goodies!

## LIGHTS
It's fab switching them on wherever you are! At home or in your town centre!

## PRESENTS
We hope you always get just what you want!

## BRUSSELS SPROUTS
Not everyone likes these. We LOVE them!

## CRACKERS
Make Christmas go with a bang! AND a joke, AND a hat, AND a pressie!

## BAUBLES
Awww! don't they look beautiful hanging on your tree?

## FROST
Crunch across this in your wellies!

## PANTOMIMES
They're fab! Oh, no they're not! Oh, yes they are!

## PAPER HATS
Wear them with pride - or a silly grin on your face!

## JOKES
The cornier, the better!

## STOCKINGS
Full of tiny pressies, open these on Christmas day!

## SELECTION BOXES
Full of our fave sweets! Chocolate heaven!

## TANGERINES
There's always one of these in your Christmas stocking! Yum!

## GLITTER
It's everywhere - on presents, on cards, on YOU! Hurray!

# Acting up!

WILL ALL NEW PUPILS PLEASE FOLLOW ME TO THE MAIN HALL?

IT was the first day of the new term at the Weston residential drama school.

ISN'T IT EXCITING BEING PART OF THE WESTON AT LAST?

YEAH! WE'RE REALLY LUCKY TO BE HERE.

I'M LUCKIER THAN MOST. AFTER THE AUDITION I WAS ONLY FIRST RESERVE, BUT THEN SOMEONE DROPPED OUT, AND I GOT THEIR PLACE.

THAT *WAS* LUCKY!

TCH! I HOPE HAVING YOU IN CLASS ISN'T GOING TO HOLD THE REST OF US BACK.

IGNORE HER! SUSIE'S A TOTAL PAIN! I'M KATY WELLS, BY THE WAY.

AND I'M AMBER FRENCH.

Katy and Amber soon became best friends —

NO, NO, NO! YOU'RE SUPPOSED TO BE CATS, NOT CART HORSES.

36

PHEW! I'M EXHAUSTED! IT'S HARD WORK BEING A DRAMA STUDENT.

HUH! WE WOULDN'T BE SO TIRED IF AMBER WASN'T IN OUR CLASS. SHE'S USELESS. THAT'S WHY MISS WESTON MADE US DO THAT SCENE SO OFTEN!

IS THAT TRUE? AM I HOLDING BACK THE CLASS, KATY?

NO WAY! MISS WESTON IS A PERFECTIONIST. IT'S NOTHING TO DO WITH YOU, AMBER!

Next morning —

COME ALONG! CLASS BEGINS IN THIRTY SECONDS! I WILL NOT EXCUSE LATENESS!

WE'RE READY, MISS.

But —

I CAN'T FIND MY SCRUNCHIE. I CAN'T GO INTO CLASS WITH MY HAIR ALL OVER THE PLACE. MISS DU PRE WILL BE FURIOUS.

SHE'LL BE EVEN MORE ANGRY IF YOU'RE LATE. I'LL TRY TO PIN IT BACK FOR YOU, AMBER.

But —

THE CLIPS HAVEN'T HELD. AMBER'S HAIR IS BEGINNING TO FALL.

AMBER FRENCH! YOU LOOK LIKE A SCARECROW! KINDLY LEAVE MY CLASS.

Later —

I FOUND MY SCRUNCHIE, KATY. IT WAS ON THE TABLE BESIDE MY BED. BUT I'M SURE I PUT IT IN MY BAG.

YOU PROBABLY JUST FORGOT. AT LEAST YOU'VE FOUND IT!

Then, a few days later —

TAKE OUT YOUR COPIES OF THE PLAY NOW, GIRLS. AMBER, YOU CAN BEGIN READING.

I — I'M SORRY, MISS, BUT I CAN'T FIND MY COPY.

THEN YOU WILL HAVE TO MISS THE REST OF THE CLASS.

THAT'S A RELIEF! WE'LL GET ON QUICKER WITHOUT *HER* HOLDING US BACK.

Later —

MY COPY OF THE PLAY TURNED UP UNDER MY BED, BUT I *KNOW* I TOOK IT WITH ME. SOMEBODY MUST HAVE TAKEN IT FROM MY BAG AND HIDDEN IT. I BET IT WAS SUSIE!

I THINK YOU'RE RIGHT, AMBER.

WELL, I'LL BE MORE CAREFUL FROM NOW ON. I'M GOING TO COLLECT TOGETHER MY THINGS FOR TOMORROW — AND SLEEP WITH THEM UNDER MY PILLOW.

GOOD IDEA! I'LL SEE YOU LATER. I'M GOING TO WRITE TO MY BEST FRIEND AT HOME.

Next day —

NOTHING WENT WRONG FOR ME THIS MORNING, THANK GOODNESS.

GOOD! WE'D BETTER HURRY, THOUGH! IT'S HISTORY NEXT AND WE'VE GOT A TEST.

Afterwards —

HOW DID YOU GET ON?

IT WAS AWFUL! I REVISED ALL THE WRONG WORK. I THOUGHT IT WAS THE CHAPTER BEGINNING ON PAGE TEN. THAT'S WHAT'S WRITTEN IN MY REVISION BOOK.

NO. IT WAS THE NEXT ONE. YOU MUST HAVE COPIED IT DOWN WRONGLY.

BUT I DIDN'T! HEY — LOOK AT MY BOOK. THE ORIGINAL NUMBER I WROTE HAS BEEN RUBBED OUT AND 'TEN' HAS BEEN WRITTEN IN ON TOP!

YOU THINK IT WAS SUSIE AGAIN?

WHO ELSE? I'M GONNA KEEP A CLOSE EYE ON HER.

But, a few days later —

WE'VE BEEN WATCHING SUSIE ALL WEEK AND SHE HASN'T DONE ANYTHING TO CAUSE TROUBLE.

MAYBE SHE'S FED UP ANNOYING YOU. YOUR PROBLEMS COULD BE OVER, AMBER.

Then —

I HOPE YOU'VE ALL REMEMBERED TO BRING YOUR MUSIC FOR THE SOLOS YOU'VE BEEN REHEARSING.

I'VE KEPT MY MUSIC SAFE IN THIS ENVELOPE. I'M STILL NOT CONVINCED SUSIE HAS GIVEN UP.

AMBER CAN PERFORM FIRST.

OKAY, MRS JAMES. THERE'S MY MUSIC, ALISON.

THAT'S NOT RIGHT! I'M SINGING FROM 'GREASE' NOT 'ANNIE'.

39

THEN WHY DID YOU BRING 'ANNIE' MUSIC TO CLASS? THIS CARELESSNESS WILL BE NOTED IN YOUR REPORT, AMBER FRENCH. NOW SIT DOWN!

OH! AMBER'S IN BIG TROUBLE NOW.

ALL THE TIME I WAS GUARDING THE WRONG PIECE OF MUSIC. SUSIE MUST HAVE SWAPPED THEM OVER *DAYS* AGO.

Next week —

THE FIRST YEAR PUPILS WILL BE PUTTING ON A SMALL PERFORMANCE NEXT SATURDAY. I WILL GIVE YOU FURTHER DETAILS TOMORROW. CLASS IS DISMISSED NOW — EXCEPT FOR AMBER FRENCH.

YOU WILL NOT BE TAKING PART IN THE PERFORMANCE. YOUR ATTITUDE HAS BEEN SO LAX AND YOUR ACHIEVEMENT SO POOR, THAT I INTENDED TO ASK YOU TO LEAVE THE WESTON.

HOWEVER, THE GOVERNORS ARE GIVING YOU ONE LAST CHANCE. THEY WOULD LIKE YOU TO PERFORM PRIVATELY NEXT SATURDAY. WHETHER OR NOT YOU REMAIN AT THE WESTON DEPENDS ON THAT PERFORMANCE.

YES, MISS.

THIS IS MY LAST CHANCE, KATY. WILL YOU HELP ME?

SURE. I'LL KEEP AN EYE ON SUSIE, TOO.

The girls remembered what happened next —

JACKIE! WHAT'S THE MATTER?

I CAN'T GO TO THE WESTON AFTER ALL. DAD'S JUST BEEN GIVEN A JOB TRANSFER TO AMERICA. THE WHOLE FAMILY IS TO GO WITH HIM.

But then, after Jackie's parents had contacted the school —

THE AMERICAN JOB'S BEEN CANCELLED. WE'RE STAYING HERE AFTER ALL.

SO I CAN GO TO THE WESTON WITH KATY? GREAT!

However, when Jackie's mother phoned —

I'M SORRY, MRS SHARPE, BUT I OFFERED YOUR DAUGHTER'S PLACE TO THE GIRL WHO WAS FIRST RESERVE, AND SHE HAS ACCEPTED IT. WE NO LONGER HAVE A VACANCY FOR JACKIE.

I WAS SO UNHAPPY THEN. BUT NOT ANY MORE. I DON'T WANT TO COME TO THE WESTON NOW.

WHAT? BUT WHY NOT?

READING YOUR LETTERS HAS MADE ME REALISE WHAT HARD WORK IT WOULD BE — ALL THOSE MOVEMENT, DANCE AND MUSIC CLASSES, ON TOP OF ORDINARY LESSONS, TOO.

JACKIE DOESN'T WANT TO COME HERE? OH, NO! I'VE MADE A DREADFUL MISTAKE! BUT MAYBE IT'S NOT TOO LATE TO PUT THINGS RIGHT . . .

# WiLD!

Nearly all of you love animals - especially cute, furry ones. But not all animals are as cute and cuddly as they look.

Lion cubs look gorgeous, but they grow to be very fierce. A male can grow to 4 feet tall and weigh 450 pounds. That's big!! Africa is the only place where naturally wild lions live today, but thousands of years ago they were found in lots of other places - including southern Europe! Erk! Imagine coming face to face with a lion on the beach!

Found only in China, pandas eat almost nothing but bamboo and, as this grass isn't very nutritious, it means they have to eat almost constantly. Maybe that's why they don't have time to hibernate. Pandas look cute, but their size makes them pretty scary. They can grow to be **enormous**.

Elephants can live until they are 70 or more - and did you know that they can laugh, and even cry? But before you start to feel too sorry for them, they can also be very dangerous. In the last 20 years approximately 20 people have been killed and nearly 100 injured by elephants.

An adult polar bear is far from sweet - standing over 9 feet tall. In fact, if a polar bear stood on its back legs it would be tall enough to look an elephant in the eye - if there were any elephants around, that is. Polar bears look white because of the light reflecting on their fur, but underneath their skin is black. Weird!

A koala isn't actually a bear, but really a marsupial, like a kangaroo or wallaby. Koalas can be very fierce and they tend to stink because of their diet of eucalyptus leaves. Yes, they may appear sweet, but koalas aren't really all that nice to know.

The platypus, with its strange looking bill, may look funny, but it wouldn't be a laughing matter if you got too close to one. The male platypus has a sharp poisonous spur on the inside of both back legs. The toxin in these spurs is strong enough to kill a dog or to cause extreme pain to a human. Luckily for us, the platypus usually only uses these spurs to fight off other males.

The cheetah is the fastest of all animals (well, travelling without an engine, that is) and can cover the ground at speeds of up to 70 miles an hour. Cheetah cubs look very, very cute indeed but before you think about petting one, remember that the cheetah is the only cat which has non-retractable claws. Ouch!

A wallaby looks really cute - like a mini-sized kangaroo - but like its larger relative, the wallaby has a very long and strong tail. If it decided to thump you with its tail or kick you with one or other of its back legs, it would do you a lotta damage.

If it's cute you're after, then watching a mum chimpanzee looking after her baby is hard to beat. But don't get too close or you could be in big trouble. Chimps are very possessive mums and they're pretty strong, too. If they think you're posing any kind of threat to their baby, they will take action - and it's unlikely that you will win!

# WiLD! PUZZLES
## They're animal-tastic!

### CRISS CROSS

Cross out the letters that appear twice or more in these squares to reveal two popular pets.

| O | E | N | O |
|---|---|---|---|
| D | C | G | A |
| V | D | E | N |
| T | O | V | G |

| A | L | D | B |
|---|---|---|---|
| T | C | L | R |
| O | B | C | T |
| R | G | A | B |

### ODD ONE OUT

Which is the odd one out in each of these groups?

Polar
Black
Koala
Brown

Cheetah
Coyote
Jaguar
Cougar

### WHY DID THE CHICKEN...

Help Charlie and Cherry Chicken find the quickest way to cross the road by leading them through the maze.

# TWIN TIME

**A** **B** **C**

**D** **E** **F**

These six lambs look alike, but only two are exactly the same. Can you spot them?

# WHO'S WHO?

Can you recognise these unusual animals? Put the right name with the correct picture.

**Meerkat**

**Serval**

**Mara**

**A**

**C**

**B**

# HIDE AND SEEK

Solve the clues to find the animals. When you have filled in the spaces, rearrange the letters in the shaded squares to find another animal.

1. It's known for 'laughing'
2. Jerry squeaks!
3. Black Beauty was one
4. A big stripy cat
5. A horse with pyjamas?
6. An Australian wild dog
7. A grown up lamb
8. A little 'bear' from Oz

| 1. | | | | |
| 2. | | | | |
| 3. | | | | |
| 4. | | | | |
| 5. | | | | |
| 6. | | | | |
| 7. | | | | |
| 8. | | | | |

Answers on page 110

# Girl Zone

PAY HERE

HAVEN'T YOU FINISHED YOUR CHRISTMAS SHOPPING YET, B? I'M EXHAUSTED!

ME TOO, LISA. BUT I'VE STILL TO GET SOMETHING FOR DAD.

AAAAGH! MY TOES!

COME ON. LET'S TAKE A BREAK IN THE CAFE.

I'LL BE GLAD WHEN CHRISTMAS IS OVER. I COULDN'T STAND FIGHTING MY WAY THROUGH CROWDS FOR ANOTHER DAY!

NEVER MIND. ONE MORE PRESENT TO BUY, AND THAT'LL BE IT!

OH, NO! I'VE JUST REMEMBERED. I'VE SOMETHING ELSE TO GET FOR MUM, TOO!

But soon —

THAT'S IT FINALLY DONE. AND IT'S CHRISTMAS DAY TOMORROW! YE-ESS!

On Boxing Day —

DID YOU HAVE A GOOD CHRISTMAS, B?

YEAH, THANKS, JO. I GOT EVERYTHING I WANTED.

WHAT D'YOU FANCY DOING TODAY?

LET'S GO SHOPPING.

WHAT? BUT WE'VE JUST FINISHED OUR CHRISTMAS SHOPPING — AND IT WAS AWFUL!

I KNOW, BUT THE SALES START TODAY! BARGAINS, HERE I COME . . .

SALE

SALE

ARE YOU ALWAYS DRAWING STICK MEN AND WOMEN ON YOUR SCHOOL BOOKS? DO YOU MAKE PEOPLE LAUGH WITH YOUR DRAWINGS? DO YOU LOVE FUNNY PICTURE STORIES? IF THE ANSWER IS YES, THEN PERHAPS YOU SHOULD THINK ABOUT BECOMING A CARTOONIST.

# CART

A LOT OF ART COLLEGES HAVE SPECIAL COURSES IN CARTOON DRAWING, BUT MANY ARTISTS BECOME CARTOONISTS BECAUSE OF THEIR OWN NATURAL TALENT. ALL YOU NEED IS A SHEET OF PAPER, A PENCIL OR A FELT TIP PEN, AND YOU'RE OFF.

ONE OF THE BES[T] TIPS, ESPECIALL[Y] WHEN YOU'RE BEGINNING, IS TO KEEP THE DRAWING SIMPLE[.] IT CAN TAKE TWICE AS LONG TO DRAW IN LOT[S] OF FUSSY DETAIL[,] AND IT'S OFTEN THE SIMPLE LINE DRAWING THAT PEOPLE REMEMBER, ANYWAY.

OF COURSE, THE WHOLE POINT OF A CARTOON IS THAT IT EXAGGERATES SOMETHING ABOUT SOMEONE, AND THAT'S WHAT MAKES IT FUNNY. IF SOMEONE HAS LONG EYELASHES, THEN MAKE THEM *VERY* LONG, OR IF SOMEONE IS WEARING STRIPY SOCKS, MAKE THEM *EXTRA* STRIPY.

ONE OF THE MOST DIFFICULT THINGS IS ACTUALLY REMEMBERING WHAT SOMEONE OR SOMETHING LOOKS LIKE. A VERY GOOD TIP, THEREFORE, IS TO KEEP A COLLECTION OF PHOTOS AND PICTURES OF ALL KINDS OF THINGS LIKE ELEPHANTS, DISHWASHERS, CARS — IN FACT *ANYTHING*! MAKE SURE YOU KEEP ALL YOUR REFERENCE PICS IN ORDER, THOUGH, AS THEY'RE NO USE IF YOU CAN'T FIND WHAT YOU'RE LOOKING FOR.

# ON CRAZY

ARTISTS BECOME FAMOUS FOR THE CHARACTERS THEY CREATE, SO TRY TO DEVELOP A SET OF CHARACTERS THAT PEOPLE CAN REMEMBER. TRY DRAWING AN ELEPHANT WITH HUGE TOENAILS OR A CAT WITH A TORN EAR. IF YOU PREFER TO DRAW PEOPLE, YOU COULD SKETCH A GIRL WHO'S ALWAYS IN A BAD TEMPER OR A LITTLE KID WHO DRAGS A TOY AROUND EVERYWHERE.

OFTEN IT IS THE SITUATION THAT MAKES A CARTOON REALLY FUNNY, SO THAT IS WHERE YOU HAVE TO LET YOUR IMAGINATION TAKE OVER. A GIRL EATING A DOUGHNUT MIGHT NOT MAKE PEOPLE LAUGH, BUT WHAT ABOUT A DOUGHNUT TRYING TO EAT A GIRL?

DRAWING CARTOONS CAN BE REALLY DIFFICULT. YOU COULD SPEND HOURS TRYING TO DRAW A GIRAFFE STANDING ON TOP OF A GUINEA PIG, BUT IF YOU GET IT RIGHT, YOUR FRIENDS WILL LAUGH FOR AGES! AND IF YOU PRACTISE ENOUGH YOU JUST *MIGHT* END UP BEING FAMOUS!

Turn over and see how to draw a cartoon cat.

THERE ARE TWO WAYS TO DRAW THIS CARTOON CAT. THE FIRST IS BY USING A GRID.

YOU WILL NEED A BLANK PIECE OF PAPER, A PENCIL, RULER, ERASER AND SOME COLOURED PENS OR PENCILS.

1. DRAW A GRID LIKE THIS OVER THE PICTURE YOU WANT TO COPY.

2. THEN DRAW AN IDENTICAL GRID, IN PENCIL, ON YOUR BLANK SHEET OF PAPER.

3. STARTING AT THE TOP, CAREFULLY COPY EACH SECTION OF THE PICTURE IN THE CORRESPONDING SQUARE ON YOUR BLANK SHEET. IT'S BEST TO DO THIS IN PENCIL SO YOU CAN MAKE CHANGES IF YOU NEED TO.

4. FINALLY, PUT A BLACK OUTLINE AROUND YOUR CAT, RUB ALL THE PENCIL LINES OUT AND COLOUR IT IN.

5. THEN HANG IT ON THE WALL TO IMPRESS ALL YOUR FRIENDS.

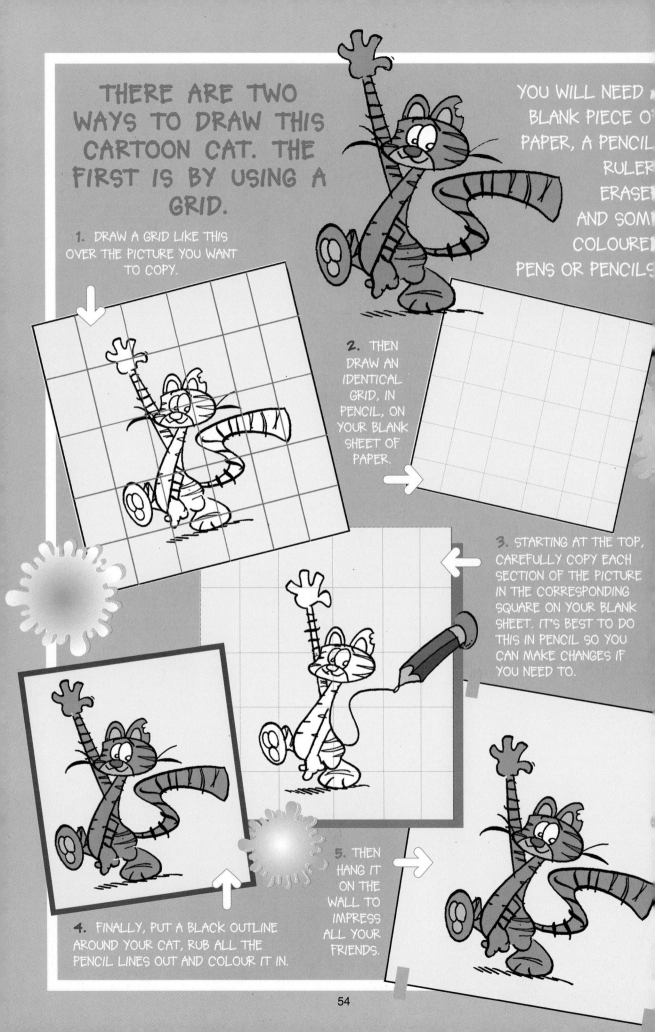

54

# THE SECOND WAY TO DRAW THE SAME CAT IS THE WAY CARTOONISTS DO IT, BY USING SHAPES.

**1.** FIRST DRAW A SLIGHTLY SQUASHED CIRCLE.

**2.** THEN DIVIDE THE SHAPE INTO QUARTERS LIKE THIS.

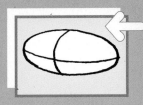

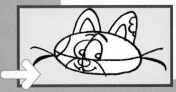

**3.** PLACE ALL THE FEATURES ON THE FACE USING THE QUARTERS TO HELP EVERYTHING LOOK EQUAL.

**6.** FINISH OFF BY PUTTING IN FINGERS AND ADDING A SWEEPING TAIL.

**4.** THEN DRAW A PEAR SHAPE FOR THE BODY.

**5.** DRAW TWO SQUASHED BALLS FOR FEET, AND STICKS WITH CIRCLES ON THE END FOR ARMS AND HANDS.

**7.** INK IN THE PICTURE, RUB OUT THE PENCIL LINES AND COLOUR IT IN...

**8.** ...THEN HANG IT ON THE WALL. WELL DONE!

YOU CAN NOW USE THIS SHAPE SYSTEM TO DRAW YOUR CAT IN ALL KINDS OF POSITIONS. TRY THESE THEN DRAW SOME OF YOUR OWN. HAVE FUN!

# Pssst!

## wanna know some stars' secrets?

**Destiny's Child** want to party with Janet Jackson!

**Jon S Club 7** would spend his last pound on a hair brush. He's obsessed with his hair.

**Kelly Greenwood** (Zara from Hollyoaks) has a tattoo of her initials in Arabic.

**Craig David** reckons he'd be a lawyer if he'd not become a pop star.

**Liz** from **Atomic Kitten's** favourite sweets are orange Smarties!

**Hannah S Club 7** is an excellent tennis player. It's her ambition to play Andre Agassi.

**Kylie's** name means boomerang in Aborigine!

Asked to describe herself in three words, **Thaila allSTARS** says she's honourable, kooky, and strong-willed.

**Sam allSTARS** loves salt and vinegar crisps.

**Hear'Say's Noel** wants to buy a yacht!

The three things that make **Shane** from **Westlife** happiest are cars, girls and horses!

Here's a quick and easy way of making funky, fun-tastic hairclips in all your fave colours!

# Go Glitter!

**you will need:**
cheap, plain hairclips
different coloured nail polish
glitter and sparkles
clear nail polish

1. Carefully paint the coloured nail polish on to the hairclips.

2. While the polish is still wet, sprinkle some glitter or sparkles over the top.

3. When the clips are dry, paint them with a thin coat of clear nail polish to seal everything in place.

It's as simple as that! Now you can have glitzy, glittery hairclips to match every one of your favourite party outfits.

All Change!

58

OF COURSE IT WON'T BE! IT'LL BE SIMPLE.

GREAT! AND I'LL BE A STUDENT AGAIN. IT'LL BE A GREAT CHANCE TO RELAX.

RELAX? WHEN YOU'RE A STUDENT? MUM'S IN FOR A SHOCK!

On the first day of the holidays —

I'M OFF! SURE YOU CAN COPE?

OF COURSE! GOOD LUCK WITH YOUR LESSONS.

STEVIE'S WATCHING TV, AND FRANCES HASN'T EVEN WOKEN UP YET. I CAN LIE IN AND READ MY MAG.

But —

JUICE! SALLY! JUICE!

OH, OH! THAT SOUNDS LIKE FRANCES NOW. TIME TO GET UP.

THERE YOU ARE! DRINK THIS ORANGE WHILE I GET YOUR CLOTHES.

But —

FRANCES! STOP POURING THAT ON YOUR BED.

TEDDY WANT JUICE, TOO.

59

TEDDIES DON'T DRINK JUICE.

EVERYTHING'S SOAKING! I'LL HAVE TO STRIP THE BED.

THERE — YOU CAN WEAR YOUR BLUE DRESS TODAY.

NO! NO LIKE BLUE DRESS!

WAAH! WAAH!

ALL RIGHT, *YOU* CHOOSE WHAT YOU WANT TO WEAR.

STEVIE, STOP FLICKING YOUR CORN FLAKES ON THE FLOOR.

THEY'RE NOT CORN FLAKES. THEY'RE GRENADES. BOOM!

MY BROTHER AND SISTER ARE DRIVING ME MAD. THEIR GAMES ALWAYS SEEMED FUNNY WHEN I DIDN'T HAVE TO CLEAR UP AFTERWARDS.

Later —

PHEW! AUNTIE KATH HAS TAKEN FRANCES OFF MY HANDS FOR A FEW HOURS, AND STEVIE'S GONE OUT TO PLAY! PEACE AT LAST!

THAT'S THE WASHING ON. NOW WHAT'LL I DO FOR TEA?

ut —

THERE ARE ONLY TWO PIECES OF STEAK IN THE FREEZER, SO . THAT'S NO USE. I'LL DO FISH INSTEAD . . .

OH, BUT STEVIE DOESN'T LIKE FISH. I'LL HAVE TO FRY HIM A BURGER. THEN WE'LL HAVE PEAS — OH AND BAKED BEANS FOR FRANCES. IT'S THE ONLY VEG SHE'LL EAT.

THAT'S ALL TOO COMPLICATED. I'LL DO SHEPHERD'S PIE FOR THE OTHERS AND CHICKEN NUGGETS FOR FRANCES.

But —

THAT WON'T WORK EITHER! THE PIE NEEDS TO BE COOKED AT 180° AND THE NUGGETS AT 220°! WHY CAN'T THEY ALL EAT THE SAME?

The Recipe Book

hen —

HEY, WHAT'S THAT SPLASHING NOISE?

OH, NO! THE WASHING MACHINE IS LEAKING! THE KITCHEN FLOOR'S SOAKED!

YES, IT IS AN EMERGENCY.

IT TOOK ME AN HOUR TO CLEAN THE KITCHEN FLOOR AND NOW IT'S TAKING ME AGES TO FIND A PLUMBER.

Eventually —

THIS WAY, MR BLEWITT.

Then —

HI, SALLY. I'VE BROUGHT FRANCES BACK.

ALREADY? I HAVEN'T EVEN SAT DOWN YET.

That evening —

NICE MEAL, SALLY. THANK YOU.

I HOPE THEY REALISE THE PLANNING THAT WENT INTO IT.

GLAD YOU LIKED IT. CAN SOMEBODY HELP ME WITH THE WASHING UP?

But —

DAD AND I ARE GOING TO WATCH THE FOOTBALL. SEE YOU!

AND I HAVE HOMEWORK TO DO. SORRY, SALLY.

OH! I CAN'T REALLY COMPLAIN THOUGH. THAT'S THE EXCUSE I USUALLY USE.

A few days later —

CLEANING, DUSTING, COOKING, WASHING, LOOKING AFTER FRANCES . . . THIS IS HARD WORK. I WISH I COULD GIVE IT UP, BUT I CAN'T LET MUM DOWN NOW.

62

# It's in the STARS!

Eyes down if you're Cancer, Leo or Virgo. Here's what's on its way in 2003.

## Cancer

### (June 22 - July 23)

Your birthday may be in the summer, but spring and autumn are your favourite times of year. Look out for extra special excitement in May. It might be connected with someone who was born under the sign of Pisces. The initial D could also bring changes for you later in the year.

### Star Special

Groovy hair accessories! You're wild!

### Hot Hobby
Tennis or shopping

## Leo

### (July 24 - August 23)

Something unexpected may crop up in the first half of the year. But don't worry, cos you'll cope with everything easily. A chance to really show what you can do is just around the corner. Don't be upset if some people are jealous, cos your real friends and family will be very proud.

### Star Special

Lovely lip balm! Mmmmmmm!

### Hot Hobby
Reading or horse riding

## Virgo

### (August 24 - September 23)

A secret you're told in January or February could be important later in the year. Make sure you remember all the details. A friend could turn to you for advice. Even if you don't agree with her, you should try to be kind. You never know, you might want advice from her sometime.

### Star Special

Chocolate, chocolate, chocolate! You looove it!

### Hot Hobby
History or cooking

more star info on page 92.

Oh, and then you walk her dog in the park, don't you? Same dull boring stuff.

What have you planned for Christmas Day, Lauren? Joe and I are going to meet up. It will be a really special Christmas for us this year!

I guess I'll just go to my gran's for dinner as usual.

Some of us are going to the Christmas Eve disco, Lauren. Are you coming?

Erm, I'm not sure, Joe. I still have to ask Mum.

And I bet she'll say no. That'll give Tara even *more* to laugh about.

Lauren was right –

No, Lauren, your cousins are coming over to see you on Christmas Eve.

Oh, I forgot.

I really like my cousins – but I wish I could have gone to the disco.

Tch! Our Christmas *is* boring! It'll be Dad snoring in front of the telly, Gran and Mum washing up, and me walking Scruffy as usual. Nothing exciting *ever* happens.

67

Ever wondered what it's like to star in a photo story? We as

### Lauren

Hi, my name's Sophie and this was my first ever photo story. I have acted before, though, as I go to a drama class. I was really pleased when the photographer asked me if I would like to take part, but I wish the weather had been a bit better - it was freezing! The funniest thing that happened was when Ellie, one of the dogs, ran off in the park. The most embarrassing? Holding hands with Ian, who played Joe. He's a mate, but I don't fancy him.

### Joe

I'm Ian and this was a great experience for me. It was a bit scary being the only boy - and I wasn't too keen on the holding hands and stuff - but we're all good mates, so it wasn't too embarrassing. I must admit that I found walking the dogs a bit difficult. Luckily their owners were always around, so I wasn't really in charge. I like both the girls, but I don't fancy either of them - which is probably just as well.

Jenna's dad and Amy's mum acted as dog handlers

**The photographer told everyone what to wear for each scen**

# e Cast!

cast of **A Very Special Christmas** to tell us all about it!

## Mum and sister

We played Lauren's mum and sister and - that's right - in real life we're Sophie's mum and little sister, Francesca. We just loved every minute!

## Extra

I'm Amy and I was in the playground scene with the others. It wasn't very much, but I really enjoyed myself. My dog, Hannah, was in more pictures than I was as she played Scruffy in the story. Ellie, who was Joe's dog, really belongs to Jenna.

## Tara

My real name is Jenna and I go to the same cting class as Sophie. I was ad excited when I was asked take part as I've never done a oto story before. I'd love to do other one, though. Playing a addie was a bit strange. I'd have preferred to be nice, I hink, but I did enjoy getting the chance to pull nasty faces.

Ian wouldn't buy a girlfriend perfume, he'd buy her chocolates.

The three leads all want to be actors when they are older.

Sophie and Jenna both appeared in a pantomime last Christmas.

Gran, played by Dorothy, put up Christmas decorations specially for the story.

Keisha Kelly says her favourite animal is a frog.

Carrots and Skippy are white rabbits and they belong to Charlotte Deakin.

carrots

Skippy

# Smart Art!

## A prize is on its way to each of the artists mentioned on this page.

Beth Kay fr
Harrogate lov
dogs and wou
like one just li
th

This tortoise was sent in by Nisha Mistry who lives in Bradford.

This cute lion cub wa
drawn by Shona from
Chippenham.

Kristina O'Neill sent us a drawing of Rock Steady. He lives at her local stables.

My favourite horse —

Rock Steady.

# BIG CRIMBO WORDSEARCH

WE'VE HIDDEN ALL YOUR FAVE CHRISTMAS THINGS IN THIS **HUGE** WORDSEARCH! CAN **YOU** FIND THEM, READING UP, DOWN, BACKWARDS, FORWARDS AND DIAGONALLY?

```
C A V J G P G R E E N R E S L
A H O L I D A Y P E B E T N I
I R Y R H Y E K R U T O E A O G
O B G I T A E G T F X D R W H
L W O N S S D N W Y I N O F T
S I L C E T I I O L N I C L S
A O D N D C M S B L G E E A E
C N T T E S T A R O D R D K M
A S G Y R Y U N S H A N I E I
N P K E R B T T L T Y X S G M
D U Z I L I R A S D R A C A O
L B A E N H G I E L S E O M T
E F S S M I S T L E T O E E N
S A E Q M G N I K C O T S S A
V L N O B B I R E K C A R C P
```

ANGEL
BAUBLES
BOXING DAY
BOW
CANDLES
CARDS
CAROLS

CHRISTMAS TREE
CRACKER
DECORATE
DISCO
EAT
FAIRY
GAMES

HOLIDAY
HOLLY
ICE
JOY
LIGHTS
MISTLETOE

PANTOMIME
PARTY
PRESENTS
REINDEER
RIBBON
SANTA
SING

SLEIGH
SNOW
SNOWFLAKE
STAR
STOCKING
TINSEL
TURKEY

# School's Out!

It was Christmas Day, Candy's favourite day of the year —

HAPPY CHRISTMAS, CANDY! WE HOPE YOU LIKE IT.

IT'S COOL, MUM. JUST WHAT I NEED FOR THE SKI TRIP.

LUCKY THING! I WISH I COULD GO SKI-ING.

YOUR TURN WILL COME WHEN YOU'RE MY AGE, KATE.

IT'S ONLY THREE DAYS UNTIL THE SCHOOL SKI TRIP TO SCOTLAND. I CAN'T WAIT.

At last the day came —

LEAVE YOUR CASES HERE SO THEY CAN BE LOADED ON THE COACH.

THERE'S MINE, MR POTTER.

WHERE'S ALI? SHE'S LATE!

HERE'S OUR LUGGAGE, SIR.

LET'S GET ON THE COACH AND SAVE A PLACE FOR ALI. WE WANT FOUR SEATS TOGETHER.

GOOD IDEA, JO.

75

Then —

MY SHOPPING BAG! IT'S GONE!

WHO'S PINCHED MY MUM'S SHOPPING BAG? OWN UP!

WHO'D WANT ANYTHING BELONGING TO FIONA'S MOTHER? INCLUDING FIONA! IT'S ROTTEN LUCK SHE'S COMING ON THE TRIP. SHE'S THE WORST PREFECT AT SCHOOL.

ALL MY MONEY WAS IN THERE! WHERE HAS IT GONE?

IF IT WAS A BROWN SHOPPING BAG, THEN MR POTTER LOADED IT ON THE COACH, I SAW HIM.

ME? OH — I DON'T THINK SO. THIS IS ALL SKI LUGGAGE.

I CAN SEE IT.

OH, DEAR! I'M VERY SORRY.

WITH 'HARRY' POTTER IN CHARGE, THINGS ARE SURE TO GO WRONG. I CAN'T THINK HOW HE EVER GOT TO BE A MATHS TEACHER.

HERE'S ALI AT LAST. OH, THAT'S ODD! HER PARENTS HAVEN'T BROUGHT HER.

DAD'S GOT A JOB INTERVIEW, SO MUM'S DRIVEN THERE WITH HIM. THE NEW PLACE IS MILES AWAY — PRACTICALLY THE OTHER END OF THE COUNTRY!

SO IF HE GETS THE JOB, YOU'LL BE MOVING AWAY?

THAT'S RIGHT. I'LL HAVE TO LEAVE ALL MY FRIENDS. IT'LL BE *AWFUL*, JO.

DON'T EVEN THINK ABOUT IT, ALI.

JO'S RIGHT. ANYWAY, YOUR DAD MIGHT NOT GET THE JOB. I BET THERE'LL BE LOADS OF APPLICANTS.

IS EVERYBODY HERE? RIGHT! WE'RE OFF!

I HOPE SO.

YE-ES!

Several hours later —

THIS IS IT! THE HOTEL LOOKS COOL. IT'S GOING TO BE A GREAT HOLIDAY!

MADE EVEN BETTER WITH A HOLIDAY ROMANCE, GIRLS. DON'T FORGET — DARREN AND I ARE AVAILABLE.

A HOLIDAY ROMANCE WITH BEN AND DARREN? THEY MUST BE JOKING!

LOOKS LIKE THOSE BOYS ARE STAYING AT OUR HOTEL. NOW THEY *ARE* SOMETHING, NATALIE.

WOW! LOOK AT THAT BLOND ONE!

In the hotel —

. . . AND MICHAEL, IAN, BEN AND DARREN ARE IN ROOM TWENTY-SIX. OFF YOU GO, EVERYONE.

PLEASE, SIR. YOU HAVEN'T CALLED OUT US FOUR.

OH DEAR, I SEEM TO HAVE MADE A MISTAKE. WAIT A MINUTE, EVERYONE. LET'S START AGAIN. FIONA, NICOLA, ANITA AND JANE ARE IN ROOM TWENTY-ONE.

But this time —

NOW I'VE TWO ROOMS LEFT OVER. THIS IS *SO* CONFUSING!

SHALL I TAKE OVER THE ROOM ALLOCATION, MR POTTER?

MISS DARBY WILL SORT IT OUT.

Next morning they had their first trip to the slopes —

YOU'RE ALL BEGINNERS, SO WE'LL START OFF WITH A GENTLE SLOPE. MR POTTER, WOULD YOU LIKE TO GO FIRST?

ER . . . YES, OF COURSE.

77

"HE'LL NEVER KEEP UPRIGHT!"

"I KNEW IT!"

"HA, HA, HA!"

"BE QUIET AND LISTEN TO THE INSTRUCTOR."

"SHOW OFF! I HOPE SHE FALLS OVER."

"NO SUCH LUCK. ME NEXT."

"YOU SHOULD KEEP QUIET AND CONCENTRATE WHEN YOU'RE SKI-ING!"

"TRUST FUSSY FIONA NOT TO SEE THE FUNNY SIDE."

"CAN I GO NEXT, PLEASE? I WAS GIVEN A BOOK ABOUT SKI-ING FOR CHRISTMAS. I BELIEVE RUNNING STRAIGHT DOWN A HILL LIKE THIS IS CALLED SCHUSSING."

Soon —

"THIS IS GREAT! I'M REALLY GETTING THE HANG OF IT."

"ME, TOO! IT'S FANTASTIC."

"TCH! I'VE HAD ENOUGH OF FIONA ALREADY! HAVING HER AROUND IS SPOILING THE WHOLE HOLIDAY."

YOU MUST ALL BE TIRED AS IT'S YOUR FIRST DAY. WE'LL MAKE THIS THE FINAL RUN.

FIONA HAS ALREADY STARTED. OH, WHAT'S THAT FANCY MOVE SHE'S DOING?

AAAGH! HELP!

THEY'RE TAKING HER OFF ON A STRETCHER. IT MUST BE SERIOUS.

But, at the hotel —

IN CASE YOU LOT ARE INTERESTED, I'VE PULLED SOME MUSCLES.

DID YOU READ ABOUT THAT IN A BOOK, TOO, FIONA?

THAT WAS A BIT MEAN.

WELL — SHE DESERVED IT! THAT'LL TEACH HER TO SHOW OFF.

CANDY'S RIGHT. AND AT LEAST IT MEANS WE'LL GET SOME PEACE ON THE SLOPES FROM NOW ON. FIONA HAS TO STAY IN THE HOTEL FOR THE REST OF THE HOLIDAY!

HEY — THERE'S THAT BLOND BOY. I'M GOING TO FIND OUT HIS NAME.

NO BOY'S SAFE WHEN NAT'S AROUND!

I WANT TO PHONE HOME TO FIND OUT HOW DAD'S INTERVIEW WENT.

79

So —

...SO THEY ASKED HIM TO START AT THE END OF JANUARY.....

YOUR MONEY'S RUNNING OUT. PUT SOME MORE COINS IN, ALI.

WHAT'S THE POINT? DAD *DID* GET THE JOB. I'LL BE LEAVING IN A COUPLE OF WEEKS.

THAT'S AWFUL!

THIS HOLIDAY WILL BE THE LAST TIME WE'RE ALL TOGETHER. LET'S MAKE SURE WE REALLY ENJOY IT!

Later —

THIS IS GREAT! I WISH I'D TRIED SKI-ING YEARS AGO.

ME TOO!

And, at the disco in the evening —

D'YOU MIND IF WE JOIN YOU, GIRLS?

ALAN AND HIS CROWD ARE FANTASTIC. THIS IS THE BEST HOLIDAY EVER!

The days flew by —

AS IT'S OUR LAST NIGHT TONIGHT, WE'LL HAVE A FANCY DRESS DISCO. YOU'VE HALF AN HOUR TO MAKE YOUR COSTUMES.

THAT'S GOING TO BE HARD.

I'LL WRAP THIS SHEET ROUND ME AND GO AS A SNOWMAN.

MY SKI-SUIT IS BLACK AND WHITE STRIPES. I'LL CALL MYSELF A ZEBRA. I'LL SEE IF I CAN MAKE A FACE MASK FROM PAPER.

Soon —

A SNOWMAN, A ZEBRA, A WAITRESS AND A PIRATE. AT LEAST WE'VE MADE AN EFFORT.

THAT'S MORE THAN CAN BE SAID FOR 'HARRY'.

WHY HAVEN'T YOU COME AS ANYTHING, SIR?

BUT I HAVE, ALISON. I'M A MATHS TEACHER.

HA, HA! I SUPPOSE HE IS!

ALAN! YOU'RE A WAITER!

YEAH! AND A WAITER AND A WAITRESS SHOULD KEEP EACH OTHER COMPANY, DON'T YOU THINK, NAT?

NAT AND ALAN HAVE REALLY HIT IT OFF.

IT LOOKS LIKE WE WON'T BE SHORT OF PARTNERS, EITHER. HERE COME THE OTHERS.

Next day —

LEAN ON ME, FIONA.

HERE'S MY ADDRESS. YOU'LL WRITE, WON'T YOU, NAT?

OF COURSE! OH, I'LL MISS YOU, ALAN.

81

**the end**

82

# Fun or Festive?

What kind of Crimbo card suits you? Try our funky flowchart and find out!

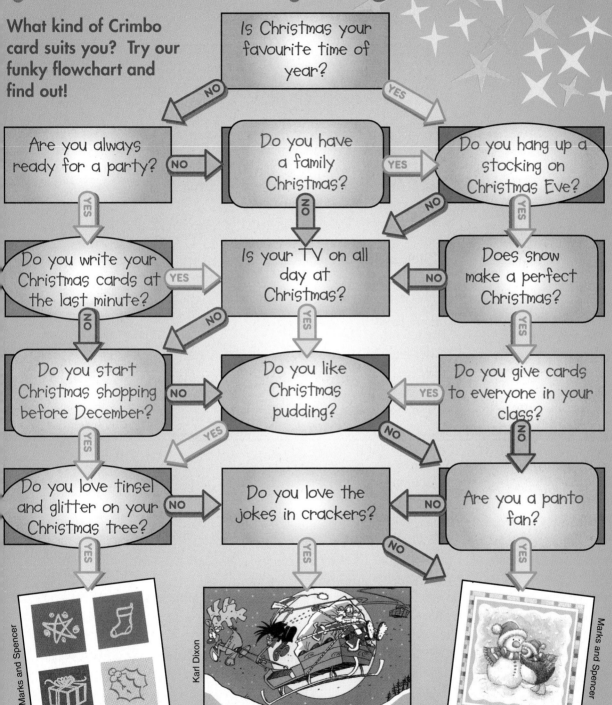

**Is Christmas your favourite time of year?**

NO → **Are you always ready for a party?**

YES → **Do you hang up a stocking on Christmas Eve?**

**Are you always ready for a party?** — NO → **Do you have a family Christmas?**

**Do you have a family Christmas?** — YES → **Do you hang up a stocking on Christmas Eve?**

**Are you always ready for a party?** — YES → **Do you write your Christmas cards at the last minute?**

**Do you have a family Christmas?** — NO → **Is your TV on all day at Christmas?**

**Do you hang up a stocking on Christmas Eve?** — NO (diagonal) → **Is your TV on all day at Christmas?**

**Do you hang up a stocking on Christmas Eve?** — YES → **Does snow make a perfect Christmas?**

**Do you write your Christmas cards at the last minute?** — YES → **Is your TV on all day at Christmas?**

**Does snow make a perfect Christmas?** — NO → **Is your TV on all day at Christmas?**

**Do you write your Christmas cards at the last minute?** — NO → **Do you start Christmas shopping before December?**

**Is your TV on all day at Christmas?** — NO → **Do you start Christmas shopping before December?**

**Is your TV on all day at Christmas?** — YES → **Do you like Christmas pudding?**

**Does snow make a perfect Christmas?** — YES → **Do you give cards to everyone in your class?**

**Do you give cards to everyone in your class?** — YES → **Do you like Christmas pudding?**

**Do you start Christmas shopping before December?** — NO → **Do you like Christmas pudding?**

**Do you start Christmas shopping before December?** — YES → **Do you love tinsel and glitter on your Christmas tree?**

**Do you like Christmas pudding?** — YES → **Do you love tinsel and glitter on your Christmas tree?**

**Do you like Christmas pudding?** — NO → **Are you a panto fan?**

**Do you give cards to everyone in your class?** — NO → **Are you a panto fan?**

**Do you love tinsel and glitter on your Christmas tree?** — NO → **Do you love the jokes in crackers?**

**Are you a panto fan?** — NO → **Do you love the jokes in crackers?**

**Do you love tinsel and glitter on your Christmas tree?** — YES → (Marks and Spencer card)

**Do you love the jokes in crackers?** — YES → (Karl Dixon card)

**Are you a panto fan?** — NO → (Karl Dixon card)

**Are you a panto fan?** — YES → (Marks and Spencer card)

*Marks and Spencer*

*Karl Dixon*

*Marks and Spencer*

You like a peaceful, old-fashioned Christmas - and you're likely to choose cards which show pretty decorations or traditional scenes. You *love* Christmas - especially if it's white!

Christmas for you is fun, fun fun! You never miss a party if you can help it and you just adore funny, cartoon Christmas cards - which you want to send to *everyone!*

You go for cute, cuddly cards every time. You want to enjoy yourself at Christmas, but you like the traditional things, too. Parties in the snow would be your ideal choice.

# IT'S GREAT

**4** Girls and mums can be great mates! Boys just see their mums as people who make meals and iron clothes!

**5** Girls used to be behind boys in the brain stakes, but not any more. We're now brainier than boys - it's official!

**6** We have hours of fun with our hair! We can wear all sorts of clips and accessories.

**7** If girls fall out with mates, we're not afraid to say we're sorry and make up again. Boys think that's soppy, and stay in the huff!

**8** Girls find it easier to make new friends because we're better at chatting to other girls. Boys are often a bit shyer!

**9** Girls can talk to mates about anything, no matter how strange! Lads just talk about football, Playstation games and, em, football!

**10** We girls can make up dance routines with o mates, give ea other mini makeovers and make yummy stuff in the kitchen!

**1** Girls get to giggle! If boys giggle, people think they're a bit mad, but it's our job to giggle tons when we're with our mates.

**2** Girls love to go shopping, even if we've got no money. Boys just don't see the point of looking at things they'd love to buy one day!

**3** When you have a best mate, she's someone you can share all your secrets with. Boys often don't have such strong friendships.

# BEING A GIRL!

## hy girls are best!

We can get way with playing l kinds of ames, like otball and omputer games. Lads don't usually like to play girlie stuff!

12 Girls can wear really girlie clothes like skirts and dresses, but we can wear tomboy stuff like trousers, trackies and chunky boots, too. Lads just don't get away with wearing dresses, do they?

13 Thanks to our mates, mums and mags, girls are much more clued up on what will happen to us as we grow up than boys are.

14 Stars like Britney tell mags how they look fantastic, so we can copy their tips. Boys don't get to do this.

15 We can sing along word-perfect to every song we love! Boys somehow don't have that knack!

16 We can wear and have any fave colour we like. Not many boys would admit that their favourite colour was girlie pink or lilac!

17 We can make our bedrooms look great with little knick-knacks and ornaments, funky posters and bright duvet covers.

18 If we're upset, we can have a good old cry and it helps us to feel better. Lads don't like crying because they get teased.

19 We get to wear great jewellery like bangles, necklaces, earrings and even toe rings!

20 We're just better than lads in every way and we have far more fun!

# SPOOKED!

**Emma and her mum had just moved house —**

Here we are, Emma, our new home. There's certainly plenty to do in the garden.

Oh, who's that, Mum?

That must be our new neighbour. Hello, Mrs Freeman.

Humph! Not very friendly, is she?

Maybe she'll be better when she gets to know us.

I doubt it! And her cat looked spooky, too.

Later —

Aaargh! What was that noise? I bet it was that scary cat again. I wish it'd stay in its own garden.

The Jones family on the other side were more friendly –

Mrs Freeman is weird. The people who used to live in your house said she put a curse on them.

What? Really?

Yeah! Everything went wrong for them after Mrs Freeman saw the son throwing stones at her cat.

We reckon the cat only stays with the old woman because she's a witch.

Oh, Dave. That's going a bit far.

But it preyed on Emma's mind –

There's that creepy cat again. I just hope Mrs F doesn't put a curse on us because she knows I don't like her cat.

Little things started to go wrong –

Another light bulb's gone! That's about the fourth this week. I'd better get the wires checked out.

I hope it's nothing to do with Mrs Freeman.

Mum tried to be neighbourly –

Hello, Mrs Freeman. How are you today? I ...

Don't bother, Mum. She doesn't want to talk to us.

87

Then, a few days later –

I – I went round to see Mrs Freeman this morning, love, and she had collapsed. I sent for an ambulance, but she died this afternoon.

Oh, Mum. That must have been a shock!

She – she asked me to look after her cat, Lady. I've searched and searched, but I can't find her anywhere.

Maybe she's gone back to the wild. She was never very friendly.

I'll leave out some milk – just in case she comes round. She must be hungry.

A few nights later –

Lady still hasn't shown up. Maybe she's gone to find another witch.

Then –

What's that? Who's moving around in the attic? Who is it? MUM!

What if it's Mrs Freeman's ghost, come to haunt me because I wasn't nice to Lady?

Don't be silly, Emma. I'll take a look to set your mind at rest.

88

THE END

# CHRISTMAS Cr

Wow!

## Crimbo Curl!

In this puzzle the last letter of each answer is the first letter of the next answer - cool! We've started you off with the first letter.

1. Pull this for a big bang! (7)
2. A small red-breasted bird (5)
3. The month before December (8)
4. Rudolph is one (8)
5. Tie up your presents with this (6)
6. Happy _ _ _  _ _ _ _ (3,4)

1.
2.
3.
4.
5.
6.
7.
8.

## Presents

**Cross out the letters which appear twice in each square a you'll reveal four fab presents**

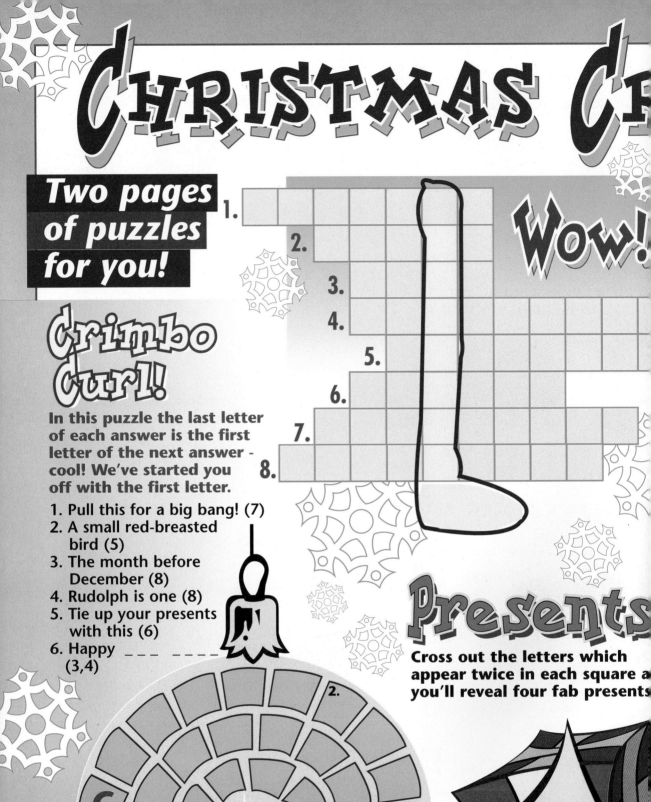

1. C
2.
3.
4.
5.
6.

```
A C F V M
U I N S L
M F P W D
U P C E U W
P C E U W
O L N A S
```

# CKERS!

## Tree-mendous!

Will **A, B, C or D** lead you to the star at the top of the tree?

ot the answers to the clues into the grid on e left and another word will appear in the aded stocking area - wow!

A red-nosed reindeer (7)
She sits at the top of your tree (5)
Decorate this with baubles, lights and tinsel (4)
A plant under which to kiss (9)
These animals pull Santa's sleigh (8)
Drape this around your tree (6)
A fun family show (9)
The season to be jolly (9)

## HO! HO! HO!

How many words of three letters or more can you make from the letters in these words?

**MERRY CHRISTMAS**

**SCORES**
20-30 fairy good!
31-40 santa-stic!
41+ you're a cracker!

A   B   C   D

## Name Game!

Unravel these letters to reveal two Christmas names - one is a boy's and one is a girl's.
**OLEN   YOHLL**

D P M I X
O L C U H
R I D B O
X S H T B
M T C L E

E F O I W
J K A R P
R T G V K
P I V C E
H G J O F

U D E B L
C H I V O
A O K U T
K E L T R
B H V Y C

*ANSWERS ON PAGE 110*

# It's in the STARS!

It's time for Libra, Scorpio and Sagittarius to see what 2003 has in store for them.

## Libra

**(September 24 - October 23)**

It looks like your popularity could reach an all time high in May - and a holiday looks like being something to remember, too. A new hobby or after-school club could lead to new and exciting friendships. But don't get carried away and forget about your old, loyal friends, will you?

### Star Special

Photo frames, for all your fave photos.

### Hot Hobby
Painting or pottery

## Scorpio

**(October 24 - November 22)**

Anything you want can be yours this year - but you'll have to work hard fo it. Be careful not to offend a friend th summer. You might think you are bein funny, but they may not see the joke Take time to sort out your finances i September. You'll need extra cash fo Christmas.

### Star Special
Your fluffy friends!

### Hot Hobby
Skating or athletics

## Sagittarius

**(November 23 - December 22)**

Winter is your favourite time of year, and both the beginning and end of 2003 look like they could be great. The rest of the year could spring surprises, too, with an exciting, outdoor type holiday a possibility. Watch out for a misunderstanding with a friend around April, though. Be warned!

### Star Special
Your address book! You'd be lost without it!

### Hot Hobby
Walking or singing

more on page 117.

Picture posed by model

# It Happened to Me...

I loved my birthday. It was my day and Mum let me do exactly what I wanted – I always said that was my best present. But last year Mum announced that she would be away with her work for a few days over my birthday.

"I've arranged for you to stay with your Aunt Paula.' Mum said. "She'll take you to school in the morning and..."

"Oh, no!" I gasped. "Her twins won't give me a moment's peace. Please, Mum! Don't make me stay with Aunt Paula on my birthday! Please!"

But it was no use. I was going to spend my birthday with Aunt Paula and Uncle Dave and their four year old twins. There would be no 'best present' this year!

Two days before my birthday Mum dropped me off.

'I'll only be away for four days,' she said, " so we can have a special celebration on Saturday."

"Huh!" I huffed. "If I can't celebrate on the actual date, then I don't see the point in celebrating at all." And with that I dashed upstairs. I was sure Mum could have got her work to change dates if she had wanted. She was just being awkward and selfish!

Over the next few days I hardly spoke to Aunt Paula or Uncle Dave and I totally ignored the twins, even although they were desperate to play with me. And on my birthday I just threw my presents on the bed and refused to open any of them. My birthday had been ruined, so what was the point in me pretending I was happy?

Then, just before tea, Aunt Paula came upstairs with the twins.

"We've brought a special surprise for you," she smiled, holding up a cake.

"We put the candles on top," the twins squealed.

"Blow them out, Kate. Blow them out!"

"I don't want to," I snapped. " And I don't want a stupid cake! Mum's ruined my birthday, so there's nothing you can do about it!"

It was then I realised that I had gone too far.

Aunt Paula blew out the candles and told the girls to go downstairs. Then she started!

"I have never, in all my life, met such a selfish girl," she said. "You've been rude to your uncle and me ever since you arrived, but this is the limit!"

"I - I'm sorry," I stammered. "But I....."

"But nothing!" Aunt Paula interrupted. "It's time you were told the truth about where your mum really is."

"What?" I gasped.

"She's not at work," Aunt Paula explained more gently, "she's in hospital, having a small operation. She lied rather than upset you, but I think it would have been easier on everyone if you had known the truth. Now don't worry," she went on, "because I've just phoned the hospital, and the operation went well. She's going to be okay."

I didn't know what to say. I'd thought Mum was being selfish, when all the time she had been ill. Now I could see that it was me who had been the selfish one. I hadn't given one thought to anyone else. All I cared about was getting my own way.

Aunt Paula was really nice to me after that – and I tried hard to help her and play with the twins. In fact, we had great fun lighting and blowing out the candles on my cake. It maybe wasn't the birthday I had wanted, but I had learned a lesson and, more importantly, I knew Mum was going to be okay. That was the best present of all.

# Sleepover Chal

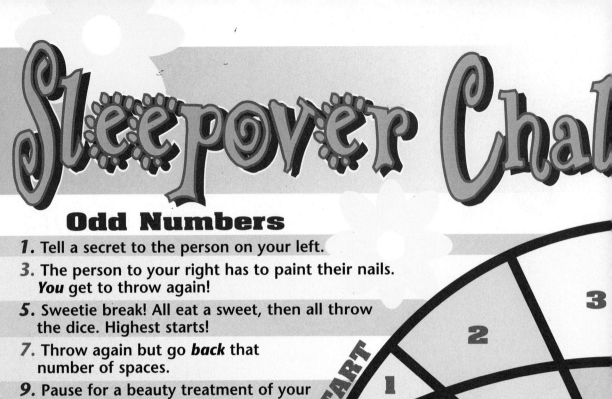

## Odd Numbers

**1.** Tell a secret to the person on your left.

**3.** The person to your right has to paint their nails. *You* get to throw again!

**5.** Sweetie break! All eat a sweet, then all throw the dice. Highest starts!

**7.** Throw again but go *back* that number of spaces.

**9.** Pause for a beauty treatment of your own choice.

**11.** Tell everyone your favourite joke. If they all laugh, throw again!

**13.** The person to your left must throw but *you* move on that number of spaces while she paints her toe nails!

**15.** Throw again but go *back* that number of spaces.

**17.** Blindfold a friend and see if she can guess two flavours of crisps. If so, she gets to throw again!

**19.** Remove an item of clothing! (You can be excused if you're only wearing a nightie or pyjamas!)

**21.** Make up a wacky dance to a song of your friends' choosing. If they like it, you can throw again — twice!

**23.** Remove an earring or other accessory. (Remember where you put it!)

**25.** Cake break! All nibble on a cake, then throw the dice. Lowest starts this time!

**27.** Play a quick game of I-Spy. If you guess the item in less than thirty seconds, throw again!

**29.** Guess the identity of someone you all know in less than ten questions. The person on your left will decide who that person is.

**31.** Dance break! All dance to your fave song, then rest.

**END — You *are* a gorg**

Grab your pals, some food, drinks, music, pens and paper and take our sleepover challenge! It's a laugh!
Highest throw of the dice starts. When you land in an area, you have to do what it says before the next person can throw. You must throw the exact number to finish. Have fun!

## Even Numbers

**2.** Pause to put on some gorgeous lipstick.

**4.** You have one minute to give yourself an interesting hairstyle!

**6.** Curl your eyelashes and nominate a pal to take another throw!

**8.** Mini karaoke — sing the chorus of your favourite song perfectly!

**10.** Everyone must write down a secret and pass it to the person on their right. (They don't have to be read out!)

**12.** Hair break! Everyone should try to put their hair up, using only clasps.

**14.** Throw again but go **back** that number of spaces.

**16.** Nominate a pal to have her nails painted — by you!

**18.** You have two minutes to give the person on your left an interesting hairstyle!

**20.** Drink break! All have a sip of your fave drink, then throw the dice. Highest starts!

**22.** You have thirty seconds to apply mascara — neatly!

**24.** Biscuit break! All eat a biscuit, then throw the dice. Highest starts — again!

**26.** Blindfold a friend and see if she can tell two flavours of fizzy drink. If so, she gets to throw twice.

**28.** You have a minute to put eye make up on the person to your left!

**30.** Try to guess how long a minute is. Get a friend to check with a watch.

**32.** Final finishing touches must now be made to your sleepover style. You want to be a gorgeous girlie winner!

e winner! Well done!

# Sisters of Sadness

EMILY and Olivia Harcourt left Victorian England to live in India with their parents where their father worked as a doctor. When both parents died during a fever epidemic, the girls were taken to a convent to be cared for by the nuns.

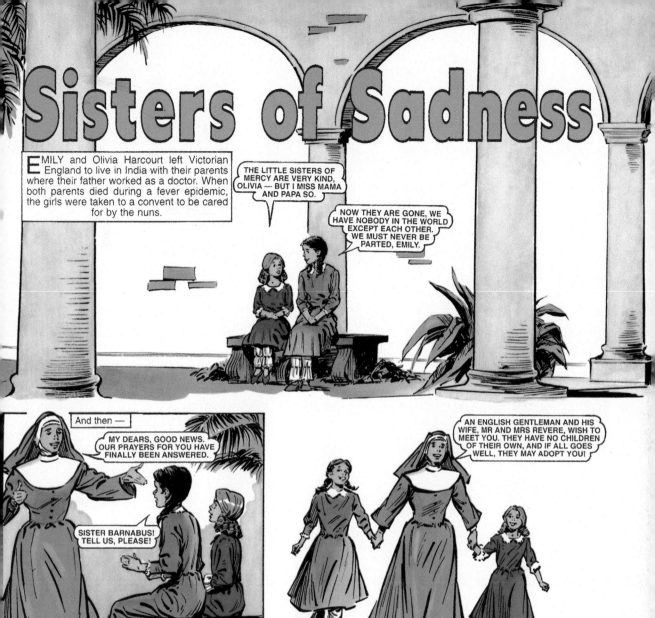

THE LITTLE SISTERS OF MERCY ARE VERY KIND, OLIVIA — BUT I MISS MAMA AND PAPA SO.

NOW THEY ARE GONE, WE HAVE NOBODY IN THE WORLD EXCEPT EACH OTHER. WE MUST NEVER BE PARTED, EMILY.

And then —

MY DEARS, GOOD NEWS. OUR PRAYERS FOR YOU HAVE FINALLY BEEN ANSWERED.

SISTER BARNABUS! TELL US, PLEASE!

AN ENGLISH GENTLEMAN AND HIS WIFE, MR AND MRS REVERE, WISH TO MEET YOU. THEY HAVE NO CHILDREN OF THEIR OWN, AND IF ALL GOES WELL, THEY MAY ADOPT YOU!

LOOK, REGINALD, THE LITTLE ONE IS JUST PERFECT. SHE EVEN HAS THE LOOK OF YOUR GRANDMOTHER ABOUT HER. WE HAVE FOUND OUR DAUGHTER!

MRS REVERE, I MUST REMIND YOU THAT THERE ARE TWO SISTERS. THEY WILL NOT BE PARTED.

JUST A SLIP OF THE TONGUE, SISTER BARNABUS. NOW WE HAVE MET THE GIRLS, WE WOULD LIKE TO OFFER THEM BOTH A HOME.

THANK GOODNESS. I WOULD NOT HAVE GONE WITHOUT YOU, OLIVIA.

MAY I SUGGEST THE GIRLS STAY WITH YOU BEFORE THE ADOPTION IS FINALISED, TO MAKE SURE YOU ARE ALL SUITED?

OF COURSE! BUT I JUST KNOW WE'LL BE ONE BIG HAPPY FAMILY.

YOU MUST ASK FOR ANYTHING YOU WANT. WE WISH ONLY TO SEE HAPPINESS ON YOUR LITTLE FACES.

YOU HAVE ALREADY BEEN TOO GOOD TO US, SIR. OUR ROOM IS WONDERFUL.

AND OUR NEW CLOTHES.

SIT HERE BY ME, DEAREST.

I THINK MRS REVERE FAVOURS EMILY, BUT MAYBE IT'S BECAUSE SHE IS THE BABY. I MUST BE GLAD FOR HER IF IT HELPS HER GET OVER THE LOSS OF MAMA.

Time slipped by and the adoption papers were duly signed.

NOW YOU ARE OFFICIALLY OUR DAUGHTERS, SO YOU MUST TRY TO CALL US MAMA AND PAPA. IT WOULD MAKE US VERY HAPPY.

I AM ONLY SAD THAT WE WILL PROBABLY NEVER SEE ENGLAND AGAIN.

However, a few days later —

WE ARE RETURNING TO ENGLAND, TO OUR FAMILY HOME, REVERE HALL. I HAVE HAD ENOUGH OF THIS CLIMATE.

MAMA, THAT'S WONDERFUL!

NOW I CAN BE TRULY HAPPY.

And on the day they sailed —

SISTER BARNABUS! YOU CAME TO SEE US OFF!

I, TOO, WILL BE RETURNING TO ENGLAND IN A FEW WEEKS. HERE IS MY ADDRESS, SHOULD YOU WISH TO GET IN TOUCH. BE HAPPY, MY DEARS.

After a long voyage, they finally arrived at their new home.

REVERE HALL IS SO OLD, BITS OF IT ARE FALLING DOWN.

HUSH, EMILY. YOU MUST NOT SPEAK LIKE THAT ABOUT MR AND MRS REVERE'S FAMILY HOME. IT IS DISRESPECTFUL.

I AGREE WITH YOU, EMILY. THE PLACE IS IN NEED OF REPAIR. SOON WE WILL HAVE THE MONEY TO BEGIN THE WORK, THANKS TO A LITTLE IDEA OF MINE!

MY DEAR HUSBAND IS SO CLEVER!

THIS IS YOUR ROOM, EMILY. YOUR SISTER'S IS UP ON THE NEXT FLOOR.

BUT WE'VE NEVER BEEN PARTED. THERE IS ROOM FOR TWO BEDS IN HERE.

IT'S TIME YOU GREW UP AND LEARNED TO MANAGE WITHOUT YOUR SISTER. YOUNG LADIES OF QUALITY ALWAYS HAVE THEIR OWN PRIVATE ROOMS. NOW WE ARE BACK IN ENGLAND, WE MUST KEEP UP APPEARANCES.

In Olivia's room —

YOUR ROOM ISN'T AS NICE AS MINE. IT'S SHABBY.

I DARESAY THEY'LL SMARTEN THINGS UP FOR ME WHEN THEY CAN AFFORD IT.

THIS IS YOUR GOVERNESS, MISS BEALE, EMILY. WHILE YOU ARE STUDYING, OLIVIA WILL LEARN SOME SIMPLE NEEDLECRAFT. SHE IS TOO OLD FOR LESSONS.

I DARE NOT COMPLAIN, BUT THIS IS VERY DULL. ALL I SEEM TO DO IS REPAIR BED LINEN.

EMILY HAS A PLEASANT TIME WITH MISS BEALE, THOUGH. TODAY THEY ARE HAVING A NATURE WALK. I ENVY MY LITTLE SISTER THAT LOVELY FRESH AIR.

TODAY WE GATHERED PLANTS AND DREW PICTURES OF THEM.

THAT SOUNDS AMUSING.

But then —

UURGH . . .!

CLUMSY CHILD! THOSE ARE NOT THE MANNERS WE EXPECT FROM OUR DAUGHTERS.

LEAVE THE TABLE AT ONCE. YOU CAN EAT IN THE SERVANTS' QUARTERS, BELOW STAIRS.

SHE JOGGED MY ARM! SHE CAN'T HAVE REALISED WHAT HAPPENED.

Several days later —

COOK, I HAVE HAD ALL MY MEALS DOWN HERE FOR A WEEK. WHEN MAY I RETURN TO THE DINING ROOM?

NEVER! THE MISTRESS DON'T WANT YOU TEACHING MISS EMILY ANY OF THEM BAD TABLE MANNERS.

YOUR NEW DRESS MAKES YOU LOOK AS PRETTY AS THIS PICTURE. THIS IS PAPA'S MOTHER WHEN SHE WAS A YOUNG GIRL. SEE IF YOU CAN COPY HER SMILE.

I HOPE SHE DOESN'T TURN EMILY INTO A VAIN LITTLE GIRL. MAMA WOULD NOT HAVE LIKED THAT. PERHAPS I SHOULD SAY SOMETHING.

I MEAN NO IMPERTINENCE, BUT OUR OWN MAMA WOULD NEVER HAVE ALLOWED EMILY TO PREEN BEFORE THE MIRROR.

OH, YOU WICKED CHILD TO SPEAK TO ME SO!

OLIVIA COMPARED ME WITH HER MAMA! SHE SAID I AM NOT BRINGING UP EMILY PROPERLY!

THERE, THERE, DEAR BEATRICE. I FEAR JEALOUSY IS THE ROOT OF THIS. OLIVIA WILL BE LOCKED IN HER ROOM AS A PUNISHMENT.

Much later —

A NOTE! IT MUST BE FROM EMILY. AT LEAST SHE HASN'T FORGOTTEN ABOUT ME AS EVERYONE ELSE HAS DONE. I HAVE HAD NOTHING TO EAT ALL DAY.

But —

Dear Sister
I think it was bad of you to make our new Mama cry when all she wants is our happiness.

I AM BEGINNING TO FEEL FRIGHTENED. EMILY AND I ARE BEING PARTED GRADUALLY, AND NOW SHE THINKS BADLY OF ME.

Next day —

I MUST NOT GIVE THEM ANOTHER EXCUSE TO SEND ME AWAY. FROM NOW ON I WILL STAY QUIET AND SAY NOTHING TO OFFEND.

But —

YOUR ATTITUDE IS DOWNRIGHT SULLEN AND INSOLENT, YOUNG LADY. I WILL NOT HAVE SUCH BEHAVIOUR IN HERE. YOU WILL REMAIN BELOW STAIRS WITH THE SERVANTS UNTIL I SEE A CHANGE FOR THE BETTER IN YOU.

BUT . . . BUT . . .

THE MASTER SAYS YOU ARE TO START EARNING YOUR KEEP, SO YOU CAN BEGIN BY MOPPING THAT FLOOR. THEN THERE'S THE PANTRY TO BE SCRUBBED OUT.

IT'S BEEN WEEKS SINCE I WAS ALLOWED OUT OF THE KITCHEN. I'M DESPERATE TO SEE EMILY. I'LL TIPTOE UPSTAIRS NOW WHILE I HAVE THE CHANCE.

Upstairs —

ALL GOES TO PLAN, BEATRICE. NOW IS THE TIME TO CONTACT THE FAMILY SOLICITOR AND INVITE HIM TO MEET OUR DAUGHTER.

ALL TRACES OF THE OTHER BRAT HAVE BEEN REMOVED. JUST KEEP LITTLE EMILY SAFE AND HAPPY UNTIL AFTER THE SOLICITOR'S VISIT — BUT THEN WHO KNOWS WHAT DREADFUL FATE MAY WELL AWAIT HER?

IT'S PLAIN THAT EMILY IS IN DANGER, BUT WHAT CAN I DO? THE REVERES WATCH HER ALL THE TIME.

Olivia wasted no time —

COME WITH ME, EMILY. DON'T EVEN STOP TO GET YOUR COAT. I'LL EXPLAIN LATER, BUT JUST RUN FOR YOUR LIFE!

WHAT ARE YOU DOING? COME BACK HERE!

But —

YOU ARE NOT LEAVING US UNTIL I SAY SO!

At that moment —

DON'T LAY A HAND ON THOSE CHILDREN!

SISTER BARNABUS! THANK GOODNESS YOU GOT MY LETTER.

Later, in the safety of the convent —

MR REVERE'S UNCLE WAS RICH, BUT AS MR REVERE WAS A GAMBLER THE UNCLE LEFT EVERYTHING TO ANY CHILD THE REVERES MIGHT HAVE. THEY CLAIMED THEY HAD A DAUGHTER BUT THE SOLICITOR INSISTED ON SEEING HER FOR HIMSELF.

THIS MEANT THEY HAD TO FIND A DAUGHTER OF THE RIGHT AGE IMMEDIATELY. EMILY FITTED THE BILL. BUT THEY HAD TO TAKE YOU TOO, OLIVIA — LUCKILY FOR YOUR SISTER! FOR THEIR PLANS INCLUDED DOING AWAY WITH THEIR 'DAUGHTER' ONCE THEY HAD CONTROL OF THE MONEY.

WE WEREN'T MEANT TO HAVE ANOTHER CHANCE OF A HAPPY FAMILY AFTER ALL.

HAVE FAITH, EMILY. SOMEWHERE OUT THERE IS A GOOD COUPLE WHO WILL BE MAMA AND PAPA TO US. BUT, UNTIL THEN, WE STILL HAVE EACH OTHER AND THAT'S ALL THAT MATTERS!

104

**THE END**

# Pssst!

## vanna know some stars' secrets?

**Mariah Carey** once asked for cute puppies and kittens to play with during an interview.

**Shane** from **Westlife** would want a supply of chewing gum with him if he was ever stranded on a desert island! Chewing it would keep him from being bored.

**Mark from A1** is scared of moths! Aw!

The first single **Becky allSTARS** ever bought was Everything I do (I do it for you) by Bryan Adams. She used to slow dance to it at discos!

When **Kelly** from **Destiny's Child** broke two of her toes, **Michelle** and **Beyonce** decorated her plaster with rhinestones.

**Bradley S Club 7** doesn't like his eyebrows.

**Britney's** fave song that she's recorded is "I'm a Slave 4 U".

**Emma Bunton** once auditioned for a part in EastEnders.

**Craig David** used to collect stamps.

**Robbie Williams** was once an extra in EastEnders, appearing in the Queen Vic.

**James Redmond (SM:tv LIVE)** appeared in Hollyoaks as a lord who owned a castle in Ireland.

# Behind the scenes at HOSPITAL RADIO

Hospital Radio is a registered charity which, thanks to the unpaid volunteers who run the small radio stations throughout the country, brings a live personal broadcasting service to patients in hospital. Louise Keogh had always wanted to see how radio worked, so we took her along to the studios of her local station.

*Well, here goes! From outside it looks like an ordinary house, but Louise knows better.*

*Inside, Louise's task is to check computer to s they have music she li Mmm! The quite a select*

*Louise meets Roy, who is DJ for the day.*

*At last it's time for Louise to get involved in the action, so headphones on and she's off.*

*Louise is a guest DJ on Roy's show. There are three mikes so there can be more than one guest at a time.*

Then the difficult bit – finding the right CD. The station carries all types of music – from pop to classical – as the age of the listeners varies all the time. It's just as well Roy's on hand to help Louise with her search.

It's serious work, but Louise turns out to be a natural. Watch out, Sara Cox!

Phew! Now for a well-deserved cuppa. "It's been a great day," says Louise. "Thanks, Roy!"

# Munch

## Ham

Ham goes really nicely with soft white bread or rolls. Or try using bagels. They're tasty and very filling. Chop the ham and mix with one dessertspoonful of mayonnaise. Add a little mustard and a chopped cornichon or gherkin. Spread over the bread and prepare to munch!

## Banana

Bananas make a really versatile filling - and can be mixed with lots of goodies.

Use nice brown bread or wholemeal rolls and spread one side with a layer of crunchy **peanut butter**. Slice the banana on top, then spread the top layer of bread or roll with more peanut butter and place over the banana. Mmmm!

### Variations

Mash a banana till it's soft then add a few sultanas and spread over the bread. For a really special sandwich, try adding some **chocolate chips** to mashed banana and then spreading the mixture onto a sesame seed roll or piece of French bread. Delicious!

## Tuna

Try tuna packed into split pitta bread or piled in a ciabatta roll. It's wild!

Drain a can of tuna and mix with a little mayonnaise. Add a pinch of chilli or curry powder and some finely chopped celery. Pile into your chosen bread or roll - and scoff!

### Variations

Add some **sweet corn** to your basic tuna and mayonnaise mix. This is especially tasty with brown or wholemeal bread. Or try mixing your tuna with **cottage cheese** and **chives** (or spring onions).

Bored with plain old ham or cheese sandwiches? Don't despair cos we've got some fabby hints to brighten up your fave fillings!

## Variations

Omit the mustard and add a little chopped **spring onion** instead. If using bagels, split an onion bagel and spread one side with your chosen spread, then lay the ham on top. Spread the other side with mayonnaise and finally spread a little mustard over the ham. Sandwich both sides together and eat.

## Cheese

Cheese goes well with most breads, but often needs a little something added to make it more exciting. Here are a few of our suggestions. Take a soft flaky croissant and spread one side with a layer of marmalade (or jam). Slice your favourite cheese and lay it on top. Outstanding!

## Variations

Spread a slice of white bread with **mayonnaise** and another with your favourite spread. Layer thinly sliced cheese, **tomato** and **cucumber** on top of one slice, season and top with the remaining slice of bread. Looks and tastes great!

Always ask an adult's permission before using kitchen equipment.

## A Little Extra

*Spread your bread with butter then top with some thinly sliced apple and chopped dates. Cover with another slice of bread and eat immediately.

*Split a ciabatta roll (or slice of French stick) and lightly toast. Rub a clove of garlic over the bread while it's warm and top with thinly sliced tomato, pepper and a little olive oil. Yummy!

*Cinnamon toast is a really special treat. Toast one side of bread then, while still warm, butter the other side and sprinkle a mixture of caster sugar and cinnamon over the butter. Pop the bread back under the grill (buttered side up) and heat until the topping starts to bubble (but not burn). Eat as soon as it's cool enough. De-licious!

Remember, there are lots of lovely breads in the shops. The right bread can make all the difference to a sandwich and make even the most ordinary filling seem exciting.
Happy munching!

# PUZZLE ANSWERS

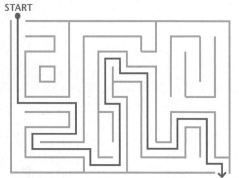

## WiLD!

### CRISS CROSS!
a) dog  b) cat

### HIDE AND SEEK
pages 48 & 49

Hyena, mouse, horse, tiger, zebra, dingo, sheep and koala. The hidden animal is elephant.

### WHY DID THE CHICKEN . . .
This is the quickest way across the road.

START

## BIG CRIMBO WORDSEARCH
page 73

```
C A V J G P G R E E N R E S L
A H O L I D A Y P E B E T N I
R Y R H Y E K R U T O E A O G
O B G I T A E G T F X D R W H
L W O N S S D N W Y I N O F T
S I L C E T I I O L N I C L S
A O D N D C M S B L G E E A E
C N T T E S T A R O D R D K M
A S G Y R Y U N S H A N I E I
N P K E R B T T L T Y X S G M
D U Z I L I R A S D R A C A O
L B A E N H G I E L S E O M T
E F S S M I S T L E T O E E N
S A E Q M G N I K C O T S S A
V L N O B B I R E K C A R C P
```

## Switched On!
page 20

### TWIN TIME
Lambs b) and e) are exactly alike.

### WHO'S WHO?
a) Serval  b) Mara  c) Meerkat

### ODD ONE OUT
Koala is the odd one out as it is a marsupial and the others are all types of bear. Coyote is the odd one out. It is a type of wild dog while the others are all cats.

## CHRISTMAS CRACKERS!
pages 90 & 91

### WOW!
1. Rudolph, 2. Fairy, 3. Tree, 4. Mistletoe, 5. Reindeer, 6. Tinsel, 7. Pantomime, 8. Christmas.

The word in the shaded area is PRESENTS.

### CRIMBO CURL!
1. Cracker, 2. Robin, 3. November, 4. Reindeer, 5. Ribbon, 6. New Year.

### PRESENTS!
1. Video, 2. Purse, 3. Watch, 4. Diary.

### NAME GAME!
Noel and Holly are the two Christmassy names.

### TREE-MENDOUS!
D will lead you to the star at the top of the tree.

# The Four Marys

The Four Marys, Raddy, Simpy, Fieldy and Cotty, were all looking forward to the Christmas holidays —

THAT'S MUM AND DAD NOW, GUYS. HAVE A GREAT CHRISTMAS AND I'LL PHONE YOU ALL SOON.

'BYE, SIMPY. HAVE A GOOD HOLIDAY.

WHAT TIME DID YOU SAY OUR TAXI IS ARRIVING, COTTY?

IN FIVE MINUTES. THAT SHOULD GET US TO THE STATION IN PLENTY TIME TO CATCH OUR TRAINS.

I CAN'T WAIT TO GET HOME. MY BROTHERS WILL BE BACK FROM UNI, TOO.

Soon —

'BYE! SEE YOU!

AH, THERE YOU ARE, RADLEIGH.

I'M AFRAID YOUR FATHER HAS CALLED TO SAY HE AND YOUR MOTHER ARE STRANDED IN SOUTH AMERICA BECAUSE OF A STRIKE.

OH, SO WHO'S PICKING ME UP?

NO ONE, AT THE MOMENT. YOU'RE TO STAY HERE AT SCHOOL UNTIL FURTHER NOTICE.

TCH! I DON'T SEE WHY I CAN'T JUST GO HOME. MY BROTHERS WILL BE THERE SOON, AND STAYING HERE ON MY OWN WILL BE DEAD BORING.

YOU WON'T BE ON YOUR OWN. I'LL BE HERE RIGHT OVER THE HOLIDAY — AND A FEW OTHER GIRLS ARE STAYING, TOO.

BIG DEAL. OH, WELL, I SUPPOSE IT'LL ONLY BE FOR A COUPLE OF DAYS. I SHOULD BE ABLE TO SURVIVE THAT!

But —

. . . SO I'M STUCK HERE WITH CREEPY. AND I DON'T KNOW WHEN MUM AND DAD WILL BE BACK!

POOR YOU! I WISH I COULD ASK YOU HERE, BUT MUM'S NOT IN AND . . .

However, three days later —

STILL NO WORD FROM MUM AND DAD. I THINK I'LL PHONE THE OTHER MARYS. MAYBE I CAN GO AND STAY WITH ONE OF THEM FOR A FEW DAYS.

NO, NO! THAT'S OKAY! I UNDERSTAND.

THE OTHERS WERE SORRY TOO, BUT IT SEEMED CHEEKY TO ASK IF I COULD STAY WHEN THEY DIDN'T OFFER.

But, later —

I CAN'T STAND ANY MORE OF THIS. I'M GOING TO PHONE HOME AND GET MY BROTHERS TO MEET ME.

TCH! IT'S THE ANSWER MACHINE. THEY MUST BE OUT.

HI, IT'S MARY! I'M COMING HOME ON THIS AFTERNOON'S TRAIN, SO CAN SOMEONE MEET ME AT THE STATION, PLEASE? SEE YOU!

So —

...AND MY BROTHERS WILL PICK ME UP. ER — MUM AND DAD ARE COMING HOME SOON.

HOPEFULLY!

BUT I WAS TOLD TO KEEP YOU HERE UNTIL I HEARD MYSELF...

ER — YOU WERE ASLEEP, MISS CREEF, AND I DIDN'T LIKE TO WAKEN YOU. IT'LL BE FINE. I PROMISE!

YE-SS! HOME, HERE I COME. I DIDN'T REALLY TELL ANY LIES, EITHER, COS THE BOYS WILL COME TO THE STATION WHEN THEY GET MY MESSAGE.

WELL...! I — I SUPPOSE IT'S OKAY. BUT MAKE SURE YOUR MOBILE IS CHARGED AND CALL ME WHEN YOU REACH HOME.

But —

OH, THERE'S NO ONE HERE. I'D BETTER PHONE AGAIN.

113

STILL THE ANSWER MACHINE. OH. WELL, I'LL JUST GET A TAXI FROM MR DAVIS.

THE PLACE LOOKS DESERTED TO ME, MISS. ARE YOU SURE YOUR BROTHERS ARE AT HOME?

YES — WELL, NO! BUT — BUT I'LL BE OKAY, MR DAVIS.

HELLO! IS THERE ANYONE ABOUT?

THIS IS AWFUL. THERE'S NO ONE HERE — AND THE HOUSE IS COLD, TOO.

AND THERE'S HARDLY ANY FOOD, EITHER. OH, WHY DID I COME?

Suddenly —

OH, NO! A POWER CUT!

I'M SURE THERE'S A TORCH OR SOME CANDLES IN HERE. PLEASE LET ME FIND THEM. *PLEASE!*

114

116

# It's in the STARS!

**Attention all Capricorn, Aquarius and Pisces. Here's what's coming to you.**

## Capricorn

**(December 23 - January 20)**
Tuesdays are your lucky days - especially in July and August this year. A move or change of school could be possible later in the year and, although you don't normally like parties or too much excitement, it looks like you could get caught up in some very special fun in 2003.

**Star Special** If it's Christmassy, you'll love it!

**Hot Hobby** Netball or reading

## Aquarius

**(January 21 - February 19)**
You might find yourself having to speak out on a subject you really care about this spring. Don't be scared - go for it! The best months for anyone born under Aquarius look like being June, September and October this year, so plan anything special for these months if you can.

**Star Special**

Bubble baths and other smelly stuff!

**Hot Hobby** Swimming or watching TV

## Pisces

**(February 20 - March 20)**
You will have to concentrate a bit more than usual if you want to get your own way this year. The colour blue could possibly bring you luck if you wear it in May or June, and a new person could bring changes to your life. Don't worry, though, cos everything will be better than before.

**Star Special** Notebooks and pens - of any kind!

**Hot Hobby** Dancing or writing

## have a cool 2003, girls!

I HEAR YOU'RE GIVING UP AS HEAD OF MATHS, MR BARKER.

THAT'S RIGHT. MR MANN IS TAKING OVER.

COOL! BORING BARKER'S LEAVING AT LAST!

GREAT! HE'S THE WORST TEACHER IN SCHOOL.

MAYBE WE SHOULD HAVE A COLLECTION FOR HIM.

EH? WHY WOULD WE WANT TO GIVE HIM ANYTHING, JO? COUNT ME OUT!

OH, I DON'T KNOW. I THINK IT'S WORTH A POUND TO SEE THE BACK OF HIM.

MMMM! MAYBE YOU'RE RIGHT, B.

So, on the last day of term —

YOU GIRLS ARE LATE! EXPLAIN YOURSELVES.

WE WENT TO BUY YOU A GOING AWAY PRESENT, SIR.

A PAPER WEIGHT. HOW NICE!

THIS WILL BE USEFUL IN MY NEW JOB.

WHERE WILL THAT BE, MR BARKER?

HERE, OF COURSE! I'M THE NEW DEPUTY HEAD — AND MY FIRST JOB WILL BE TO CRACK DOWN ON ALL LATECOMERS!

OH, NO!

On the last day —

121

Suddenly —

EEEK! THE POWER'S GONE OFF!

THERE'S A SMALL BATTERY RADIO IN THE CUPBOARD. WE CAN LISTEN IN ON THAT.

THIS IS A WEATHER WARNING. THE HIGH ROAD TO REDVALE IS UNDER SEVERAL FEET OF WATER. POLICE ADVISE PEOPLE NOT TO ATTEMPT TO TRAVEL.

OOPS! THAT'S OUR ONLY WAY OUT OF HERE, I'M AFRAID, GIRLS.

Y-YOU MEAN WE'RE STUCK HERE?

BUT IT'S CHRISTMAS EVE TOMORROW! WE HAVE TO GET HOME!

DON'T WORRY. IF THE RAIN STOPS, THE ROAD MAY CLEAR . . .

But, later —

WELL, THE RAIN'S STOPPED — BUT IT'S TURNED TO SNOW!

THIS STORM COULD GO ON FOR DAYS!

WE COULD BE STUCK HERE FOR CHRISTMAS DAY! NO FAMILIES — NO PRESENTS.

OH, NO . . .

WELL, AT LEAST THERE'S A SMALL BACK-UP GAS RING. WHO'S FOR A MUG OF SOUP?

THIS COULD BE OUR CHRISTMAS DINNER, YOU KNOW — SOUP AND SANDWICHES.

AW, DON'T, CLAIRE!

HEY, DON'T WORRY. ONE YEAR I HAD BAKED BEANS FOR CHRISTMAS DINNER!

WHAT?

122

DAD WANTED TO COOK THE TURKEY AND HE FORGOT TO SWITCH THE OVEN ON. WE HAD OUR DINNER FOR SUPPER THAT DAY!

HA, HA!

THAT WAS THE YEAR MY MOM AND CARLY WENT BACK TO THE STATES.

OOPS! I MEANT TO CHEER PEOPLE UP, NOT REMIND ROZ ABOUT HER MUM AND SISTER MOVING AWAY.

REMEMBER THE YEAR YOUR BABY SISTER WAS BORN JUST BEFORE CHRISTMAS, NIKKI?

YEAH! I BURST INTO CLASS AND TOLD EVERYONE THAT SHE WAS CALLED ELIZABETH . . .

. . . SO GRIM GERTIE SET US A TEST ABOUT ELIZABETH THE FIRST!

TYPICAL!

THAT WAS MY HAPPIEST CHRISTMAS EVER — BUT THIS YEAR IT DOESN'T LOOK LIKE I'LL BE HOME!

OH, NO! WE'RE ALL GETTING DEPRESSED NOW.

123

LET'S THINK OF SOMETHING CHEERFUL — TO KEEP OUR SPIRITS UP.

GOOD IDEA, BECKY!

REMEMBER OUR FIRST YEAR AT THE COMP, MR COLE? WE PUT ON A PANTO — ALADDIN IN TEN MINUTES!

I'D RATHER FORGET IT, THANKS!

OH, BUT YOU WERE BRILLIANT AS ABANAZER THE VILLAIN, SIR.

AND WHAT ABOUT HODGE AND FREDDY AS WIDOW TWANKY AND WISHEE WASHEE?

REMEMBER THEIR DANCE?

YEAH! PITY THEY COULDN'T!

THE BEST PART WAS YOU TWINS AS THE HORSE.

ESPECIALLY YOUR SECOND ENTRY . . .

. . . WHEN YOU EACH WENT IN DIFFERENT DIRECTIONS!

AND THE COSTUME SPLIT IN THE MIDDLE.

HA, HA, HA!

THAT WAS HAYLEY'S FAULT — AT THE BACK!

IT WAS NOT! IT WAS BECKY, AT THE FRONT!

HEY, LISTEN! CAN YOU GUYS HEAR SOMETHING?

IT'S A HELICOPTER! IS IT COMING HERE?

I DOUBT IT CAN LAND IN THIS WEATHER, LAURA.

LOOK — IN THE COPTER! IT'S *SANTA!*

HE'S DROPPED SOMETHING BY PARACHUTE!

Mr Cole went outside for the crate —

SUPPLIES! FOOD AND LIGHT FOR THE STRANDED! GOOD OLD SANTA!

AND PRESENTS!

WITH OUR NAMES ON, LOOK!

A SILVER STAR NECKLACE!

GREAT! THE HAIR ACCESSORIES I WANTED.

MMM! MY FAVOURITE SOAP!

The girls spent a happy night and, next morning —

GOOD NEWS, GIRLS! THE WEATHER'S EASED OFF ENOUGH FOR A LAND ROVER TO GET THROUGH.

WE'RE GOING HOME AFTER ALL!

HOORAY!

So, soon —

THIS LOOKED LIKE BEING A DISASTROUS CHRISTMAS — BUT IT'S BEEN REALLY GOOD FUN!

ESPECIALLY WHEN SANTA CAME!

I WONDER WHO THAT SANTA WAS?

PROBABLY SOME MEMBER OF A MOUNTAIN RESCUE TEAM.

YEAH, BUT HOW DID HE KNOW ALL OUR NAMES — AND *EXACTLY* WHAT EACH OF US WANTED FOR CHRISTMAS?

OO-ER! YOU DON'T THINK . . .

**the end**

# Are you a bathing beauty? Find out with this fun quiz!

# BaTH TiME

## 1. Which of the following do you most enjoy?

a) An invigorating shower first thing in the morning.

b) A long soak in a bath with loads of bubbles, and the latest copy of your fave mag.

c) A quick dip in the bath before going out.

## 2. On holiday in a posh hotel, which of these would you use?

b) The sauna. You love to bake in the heat, and hope that it gives you a healthy glow.

a) The swimming pool. You'd do ten lengths before breakfast almost every day.

c) The jacuzzi. You can float around a little, pretending you're being energetic.

## 3. When washing your hair for a special party, do you . . .

c) Enjoy soaking your head under the shower and blow-drying your hair into shape?

b) Spend hours with it floating behind you in the bath, letting it soak up bath essence?

a) Rinse it quickly in the sink, then leave it to dry naturally. You don't like messy conditioners and oils?